D1608150

BOOKS BY ALINA

The Frost Brothers
  Eating Her Christmas Cookies
  Tasting Her Christmas Cookies
  Frosting Her Christmas Cookies
  Licking Her Christmas Cookies
  Resting Grinch Face

The Wynter Brothers
  Good Elf Gone Wrong
  Elf Against the Wall

The Richmond Brothers
  The Art of Awkward Affection
  The Art of Marrying Your Enemy

Check my website for the latest news:
http://alinajacobs.com/books.html

HOLLY
AND
Homicide

A Holiday Cozy Romantic Mystery

HOLLY AND Homicide

ALINA JACOBS

Summary: When your cheating husband drops dead in your Christmas cat café—poisoned by your signature Santa's Surprise cupcake—things go from bad to worse. The whole town thinks you did it, including the grumpy but gorgeous lawyer guilt-tripped into defending you. Clearing your name means solving the mystery, but keeping your heart out of trouble? That's a holiday challenge you didn't see coming!

To my female ancestors of yore...
at least one of whom I am sure has
totally poisoned a cheating husband
in her day!

"What child is this..."

–William Chatterton Dix

CHAPTER 1

Emmie

"**I**f I've told you once, I've told you a thousand times—you need to keep your goddamn cats out of my establishment!"

"It's Christmas, Charles," I said, doing my best to keep up the cheery Christmas-loving facade in the face of my antagonistic next-door shop neighbor. "Let's all be a little more charitable." I took the tortoiseshell cat. "Maybe she just wants you to adopt her."

"I'd never allow one of those filthy animals in my bakery," the older man sputtered. "I come in at two a.m. to start my pastries. I don't need cat hair everywhere. The next time I see one of these vermin, I'm calling the cops!"

There were yells of surprise as a crowd of people wearing sweaters decorated with cats and carrying signs pushed through the waiting line for my popular Christmas-themed cupcakes.

"Feral cats don't belong in a café! No way!" they chanted.

"All these cats are up for adoption…" My voice rose as I prepared to have the same exact argument with my fellow feral-cat-committee members that we'd had during the last few months since I'd opened the Santa Claws Café.

Alice turned up her sharp nose. "You are using these cats for your own financial gain."

"Interacting with the customers helps them be socialized," I argued.

"This is not how the feral-cat committee does things," Gertrude, an older woman and the official chair of the cat committee, ranted. "Not to mention you have pink in your Christmas decorations."

"It's cute."

"It's not traditional. Just like this scam you're running."

"Every day, one of my customers adopts a cat," I reminded Gertrude. "The Santa Claws Café moves more cats than the Humane Society. We serve cupcakes with a side of cat!" I chirped. That was our slogan.

"Like you have people eat the poor cats," a man in a suit sneered in an unreasonably deep voice.

I glared into the crowd.

The feral-cat-committee protestors ignored me and continued to march around in a circle in the middle of my shop. I'd agonized over the decorations, the furniture, and the holiday-themed art on the walls. The café was adorned with twinkling Christmas lights, wreaths, and garlands of evergreen. The scent of freshly baked cupcakes and spiced hot cocoa filled the air. The soft Christmas music playing in the background was drowned out by angry chants. My cozy seasonal cat café was now a demonstration site.

"Do you still have Santa's Surprise cupcakes left?" one young woman called out impatiently from the back of the line. "I'm not standing here unless you do. Oh, hey, Grandma!" She waved to a velour-tracksuit-wearing woman in the pack of senior citizens crowded around the utensil station.

"Ava!" An older woman wearing knitted reindeer antlers waved.

"I'm actually here to meet her..." The young woman stepped out of line.

There were angry shouts and grumbling from the line as Ava cut around the waiting customers.

"Gran!" I yelped at my grandmother, who was coming out from around the counter with trays of coffee. "What are you doing?"

"You can't keep people waiting in line like this. You'll lose customers," she said, passing out small sips of coffee and little bites of the new cupcake recipe I'd been working on, the Sugar Plum Fairy. "You'll never have enough money to move out at this rate."

Panic set in. My heart was pounding from anxiety, or it could have just been from the sheer amount of coffee I'd consumed since five thirty that morning.

"Move out? You want me to leave?" My chin trembled. "On Christmas?"

"Can we please just order?" that same deep male voice snapped.

I ignored him. I was about to be homeless, for Kris Kringle's sake.

Gran patted me on the arm. "I love having you, but you're cutting into my sex life. And it's cutting into yours.

You'll never meet a man if you're sleeping on your grandmother's couch."

"I don't need to meet a man," I said. "I'm technically still married. My vows mean something to me, even if they don't to Brooks."

"Just kill him so you can move on!" Granny's friend Donna cackled.

I felt the anger and humiliation of the betrayal settle into a scowl on my forehead.

Gran reached up. "You don't want wrinkles. Women who are on a rocket ship to thirty-five with no kids don't need wrinkles."

That was what stung the most. Brooks and I had had trouble conceiving. We—meaning I—had spent thousands on fertility specialists, and the minute Brooks ran off to cheat on me? Bam. The homewrecker was pregnant.

"I wish he'd get run over by a herd of reindeer." I wiped at my eyes with my apron.

"You didn't need a baby with that balding Ronald McDonald anyway." Gran made a rude noise.

"Speak of the devil…" I glared at the front door.

"Don't do the devil like that," Gran said loudly. "At least Lucifer is hot and doesn't have a beer gut!"

Oakley, homewrecker extraordinaire, paraded into my own freaking café, arm in arm with my own freaking husband. Even though she had a huge eight-month-pregnant belly, she was still graceful in high heels.

Meanwhile, my face was puffier than hers, and I wasn't pregnant.

Life was so unfair.

"I don't know what you're doing in here unless it's to join with me and Emmie in plotting *his* murder." Gran jabbed in Brooks's direction with a spoon.

"Murder him when I'm not late for my shift!" one of the EMTs in line called in annoyance.

"We'll be right with you. Thank you for your patience. Pet a cat!" I called, shooing a big white Persian to go mingle with the customers.

"Cats aren't pets—they're human beings!" came the chants from the feral-cat-committee demonstrators.

"I don't know how you still have customers," Brooks sneered. "All these animals running around. And your cupcakes are infected by cats."

"Nothing is wrong with my cupcakes," I snapped. "I brush all the cats daily, and they don't come into the kitchen when I'm baking."

"Then why are these cupcakes spoiled?" Oakley thrust an open one of my café's signature red- white-and-green-striped boxes at me.

"No skipping the line!" one of my customers yelled.

"I'm not skipping the line," Oakley snarled. "I am here to lodge a formal complaint. Emmie's cupcakes are revolting. You!" Oakley pointed at a cop while Brooks convulsed in anger in front of me. "You need to shut this place down. It's a public health hazard."

Officer Winston Girthman sighed loudly and held up his hands. One cat sitting on a shelf nuzzled his hand. He petted it. "Ma'am, there is a new law on the books. Cat cafés are legal with a provisional license."

"I don't care."

"You didn't call this cop," Alice snapped at Oakley, waving the sign at her. "This is my cop. I called him, and cats are completely sanitary. No, this place needs to be shut down for animal rights violations!"

The cat purred.

"Seems like a happy cat to me." Winston, the cop, shrugged.

"She's up for adoption!" I trilled, pointing at a sign.

"I do like cats…"

"Focus!" Alice screeched.

From the crowd, there were more sighs.

A male voice complained loudly that he wished he'd stayed in New York City.

"Welcome to the quirky small town of Harrogate," I called to him. "This is all part of our charm!"

"Yeah, if you want to get poisoned," Oakley spat at the tall man in a suit. She whipped the lid off the box. "You need to be shut down for serving these to people."

Inside, two of the Santa's Surprise cupcakes were missing from the dozen, and a third had a big bite taken out of it.

I reached for one and sniffed it. It did smell a little off. Not that I was going to tell Oakley that.

"Do you have a receipt?" Gran demanded.

"Also, why are you eating cupcakes from my shop, anyway?" I demanded. "I'd never sell anything to the woman who helped my husband cheat. Did you have someone sneak in here to buy them?"

"As if I'd eat a cupcake, especially *yours*." She turned her nose up. "Brooksey says there's something wrong with the cream filling." Oakley turned to the rest of the customers, who were looking a little concerned as she held one of the red-and-white cupcakes aloft. "Be warned that Emmie's cupcakes will make you sick. Look at my poor baby." She gestured to Brooks, who did, in fact, look sick. Or maybe it was rage.

I couldn't believe that I'd loved him once. Now the man I'd sacrificed seven years of my life for looked at me with hatred in his eyes. As the star on top of this Christmas tree of betrayal, he and his homewrecking-affair partner were trying to ruin my business—the very last thing I had left, a business I'd managed to scrape together from the scraps of my ruined marriage with the last of my savings and against all odds.

"Oh yeah?" I said, trying to keep the tremble of fury out of my voice. "If they were so bad, why did you eat two of them?"

My husband went red-faced. "You're a fucking delusional cunt, Emmie. You always criticize me; you always undermine me. You're a narcissist! It's no wonder no man wants you."

"I'm a narcissist?" I choked out. "Why? Because I tried to get you to eat broccoli? God forbid there's something green on your dinner plate."

"You put bean sprouts in my sandwich," my husband said petulantly.

"They're good for you. As we get older, we need to be better about our diets." I seethed.

"See? You're nagging. This is why he left you for me!" Oakley screeched. "No man wants some woman telling him how to live his life. Just shut up and cook."

The people in line, who were only moments ago complaining about how long it was taking, were now watching the drama unfold with rapt attention.

"You're the one who's dumpy and eats too much cake anyway!" Brooks's face was almost purple as he screamed at me. "You're not supposed to get hooked on your own supply."

"That's right, sweetie," Oakley said soothingly.

"I should never have married you," Brooks spat. He was practically frothing at the mouth. "You spent all my money, you cooked food I hated, you were always the worst-looking woman at company events. You criticize everything."

"Because you're an adult toddler and can't clean up after yourself. You left your dirty clothes everywhere and tracked mud all over the floor I just cleaned. You belittled me constantly!" I cried. "Every day, you made my life miserable, and now you won't"—I pulled out a stack of papers and slammed the drawer in the counter closed—"even sign the freaking divorce papers!"

"I'm not paying you a goddamn cent!" he bellowed, slapping the papers out of my hand. "I knew the minute you didn't put out on our wedding night that you were defective. That's why you couldn't even get pregnant."

"I put out," I hissed at him. "I just refused to do—"

"Anal!" Oakley screeched at the top of her lungs while the onlookers watched in horrified fascination, phones out.

This was *so* going on the Harrogate Facebook group.

"Guess what! That's how I stole him from you. Actually, correction—he came willingly." Oakley was smug. "I believe if a man buys you dinner, he's entitled to sex."

"You see?" Brooks sputtered, the veins in his eyes almost popping. "A real woman is supportive."

"I wasted years of my life with you. I should never have married you!" I yelled. "I wish you'd just died on our wedding day."

"You're about to kill him with these cupcakes," Oakley snapped, waving the box at me. "They were revolting. Inedible. *Poisonous.*"

In the café, people had stopped eating and were looking around in concern.

"There isn't anything wrong with the cupcakes," I said, trying to keep my voice from sounding shrill.

Several people in line sidled to the door.

"Please don't leave," I begged my customers. "We have a brand-new cupcake flavor, just out last Sunday—the Santa's Surprise cupcakes."

"You mean the kind in that box?" A guy in the front of the line pointed.

There were gasps of shock from the crowd and then from Brooks.

"Poison! They're poison!" Brooks grasped the box of cupcakes, then his knees collapsed. One hand clutched his throat. The other held the box of cupcakes emblazoned with my café name.

He fell to the ground, the cupcakes tumbling out of the box onto him as he convulsed and frothed on the black-and-white-checkered-tile floor.

Blood poured out of his mouth while Oakley wailed and patrons screamed.

"Poison!"

"The food is poisoned!"

"Save the cats!" Alice cried.

"Save my baby!" Oakley wailed as the EMTs rushed in to help.

But it was too late.

I watched them work on Brooks as, around me, my livelihood went down in flames. People were throwing away their cupcakes and dumping out their coffee.

Winston called for backup on his cop radio. Outside, sirens wailed.

The senior EMT, grim faced, finally sat back on his heels, glanced up at the cop, and shook his head.

Oakley's hand fluttered to her mouth. The other flew to her huge pregnant belly. "Dead? He can't be dead."

"I think," the EMT said, looking up at me, down at the cupcakes, then back up, "he may have been poisoned."

Before I could stop myself, I shouted, "I didn't do it!"

CHAPTER 2

Marius

"Lucky duck! You only just got into town this morning, and already, Edna's granddaughter murdered her husband." Aunt Frances cackled. "This is shaping up to be a humdinger of a December."

"Indeed."

In a moment of guilt after Thanksgiving, I'd agreed to work remotely from my elderly great-aunt's guest room in the senior living complex I paid a lot of money for her to live at. Because—as Aunt Frances had tearfully declared over the Thanksgiving sandwiches she was prepping for me at my parents' house—this could be her last holiday season on earth. She had never been blessed with any children, and I was like a son to her. All she wanted for Christmas was to spend just a little more time with me before she passed.

As if.

The small older woman was spry and energetic, waving to her friend and loudly talking about the corpse on the floor like they were discussing what to bring to the holiday party.

After I'd graduated from law school, my parents had retired and started spending the majority of their time on cruise ships. I tried my best to forget about my small hometown of Harrogate. I was a big-shot corporate lawyer in New York City. I didn't need the small kooky town.

I should never have come back. My parents had the right idea—get out of Dodge for Christmas.

Now an innocent man had been murdered right in front of me.

"I can't believe Emmie would poison her husband," Aunt Frances was saying loudly.

"My baby daddy!" Oakley was screaming from the floor of the café.

The police were trying to get things under control. Good luck in the small town of Harrogate. Someone yelled out on the street that there'd been a murder at the Santa Claws Café, and townspeople came running. Several were trying to buy cupcakes because they wanted to resell them. Others wanted to know about the cupcake advent calendar.

"Do we still get our daily cupcake?" a young woman asked Emmie anxiously as the heavyset police officer tried to untangle his handcuffs from his belt.

"I don't know, Ava!" Emmie wailed. "I don't know what's going to happen!"

"Now, see here," Ida scolded Officer Girthman. The elderly woman ran the local general store and seemed to be the font of all the small-town gossip,. "Emmie did the world a solid. You can't arrest a woman for killing her cheating husband. She should be thrown a parade, not thrown into jail. I'm calling my congressman!"

Winston dropped his handcuffs.

Emmie helpfully picked them up off the floor for him, tears still streaming down her eyes.

"I spent a lot of money on that advent calendar. I need my cupcakes. I'm going to be suing the police station," Ava complained.

"Good! Arrest her!" Alice, the crazy cat lady, was screeching. "You're going to rot in jail for what you did to these poor cats! Cats belong outdoors."

"Can we go, Aunt Frances?" I begged. "We can buy a coffee next door."

It was hopeless; she ignored me, still speculating about the murder with her friends.

More people streamed into the cramped shop. I was jostled.

Moose meowed. The Bengal cat was in his harness and perched on my shoulder so he didn't get stepped on.

A pudgy, short man froze, looked up, then beamed. "Marius! You didn't tell me you were in town."

Because I'd hoped to avoid everyone I'd gone to high school with.

Abbot grinned. "Long time no see." He held up his notepad. "I work for the *Harrogate Chronicle* now! Finally got that full-time gig after old Mr. Harrison kicked the bucket. I'm so glad there was a murder. I bet papers sell out tomorrow. Shit, I gotta get the scoop. Web traffic is up. You want to give a statement?"

"No, thank you."

Abbott pushed his way through the crowd to the corpse.

"Ooh! I need to get a better view." Aunt Frances grabbed my wrist like I was five and dragged me through the surge of rubberneckers.

"I really don't want to get involved."

The police handcuffed the crying murderer.

Moose hissed when one of the café cats got too close.

"She didn't do it!" Aunt Frances's friend Edna was yelling to anyone who would listen. "My granddaughter didn't kill her husband. This is a violation of her constitutional rights."

"It's not," I muttered under my breath.

"How do you know?" Edna demanded.

"Because—" Aunt Frances began.

"No," I hissed.

"Marius is a lawyer, remember? Is the dementia setting in, Edna? My God."

"A lawyer?" Emmie croaked, looking up at me.

Maybe without all the snot and tears on her face, she might be attractive. But now…

"I don't take charity cases."

"Yes, you do." Aunt Frances poked me. "I've seen you in court—you're like a movie star! Like Richard Gere in *Chicago*."

"Please," the young woman whimpered. "I need to run my shop. I can't go to prison. I just can't. Who will take care of my cats?"

Twenty pairs of feline eyes blinked at me.

"They're used to being inside." She hiccupped. "If the café closes down, they'll have to go back outside in the cold and the snow, and they'll never find forever homes."

If I were anyone else, maybe the big, tearful brown eyes would have swayed me, but we lawyers were a sociopathic bunch.

"Hard pass."

"Of course he will. Marius," Aunt Frances said firmly and gestured to me. "Do your lawyer thing."

The elderly woman turned to the stressed officer and said loudly, "Emmie has a lawyer now. You have to let her go."

"I do?" Officer Girthman asked, confused.

"No!" one of the firefighters yelled and rolled his eyes as he and several other trooped in. The health inspector followed and began taking custody of all the cupcakes.

"Yes," Aunt Frances insisted. "You need a warrant, or you can't speak to her."

I made a helpless gesture. "That's not how any of this works."

"Marius, I expected better of you."

"Ow!" I yelped when Aunt Frances reached up to grab my ear.

"I paid a lot of money for you to go to law school. I need to see some results. There's a good boy." The elderly woman patted my cheek.

The police officer dragged Emmie to her feet. More officers were swarming in along with several bored firefighters put on crowd control.

"Can't you blow something up, Emmie?" one of them begged.

"Poisoning your husband? Lame! There hasn't been a fire all winter," another firefighter joked then grinned when he saw me. "Hey, it's Marius!"

"Luke." I nodded, shaking his hand.

"Come from the big city to grace us with your presence? We should get a beer at the Christmas market after this."

"He can't," Aunt Frances said. "He has a client to help."

"Godspeed." Luke saluted me then turned to grab a black cat off a shelf. "You aren't supposed to be here, Salem."

Resigned, I followed Aunt Frances as she power walked out of the café with the impromptu parade of police and senior citizens, down to the station along Main Street. For someone in her eighties, Aunt Frances was unreasonably spry.

Definitely has a lot more Christmases left in her. And I absolutely should have stayed in New York.

I hadn't even gotten any coffee.

No one batted an eye at Moose perched on my shoulder, because people were carrying all sorts of random shit down Main Street. In one case, a whole family was carting what looked to be a drunken uncle, who saluted me with his beer can.

As we headed down the snowy street, where it looked like Santa Claus had gotten blackout drunk and vomited holiday cheer everywhere, I tried to get into my criminal-defense-attorney mindset.

Even though I had a cushy corporate position at Richmond Electric, where I oversaw multibillion-dollar buyouts and reviewed federal contracts, Aunt Frances refused to believe that was the job of a real lawyer. She said she had paid for me to go to law school, not be a secretary, because I didn't look cute enough in a skirt for all that.

Aunt Frances and the seniors occasionally took a field trip to watch my pro bono criminal-defense cases in New York City. I'd take them to dinner on "that big lawyer salary," during which they would give me helpful tips gleaned from *Law and Order* marathons.

"You don't have any student loan debt," Aunt Frances reminded me as I dodged tourists and locals. "You're paying it forward. You remember Anya Pechowski?"

"No..."

"Yes, you do. You helped her son Alex get off on that mistaken-identity kerfuffle. She's still so grateful. You're a good person, and I know you can help Emmie."

I did not believe I could help Emmie. "The best we'd do is a plea bargain. Maybe ten years in jail, five with good behavior?"

"Don't you phone it in." She wagged her finger at me. "That poor girl needs a good lawyer. Now, her grandmother sleeps around—that's true—and her husband was stepping out on her. But the girl can cook, and she has a nice rack."

"Can she really cook if her food killed someone?" I squinted.

The police station was packed when we arrived. The officers were running around like that chicken Aunt Frances's old next-door neighbor used to have.

"Where's the murder box?" the police yelled.

This is not New York City, I reminded myself. *Shit, I might be able to get Emmie off just on the fact that no one here is following any sort of procedure.*

Aunt Frances bypassed the waiting room, scolded one cop when he meekly asked her to please not go into a restricted area, then marched right into the police chief's office.

I let her.

Emmie was huddled in a holding cell, one that looked like it was out of the 1920s, with bars and everything. Weepy, she sat across from a drunken man who was half falling off of the bench.

As much as I didn't want to help her, *couldn't* really, my brain was already cranking up, analyzing the facts of the case.

It's always the spouse, I reminded myself. *Always.*

Emmie was sobbing hysterically now.

Her grandmother clung to me.

"Help her. You have to help my granddaughter. She's soft and weak. She's not like me. She can't survive prison. I did it!" the old woman yelled. "I killed Brooks! My granddaughter had nothing to do with it. Arrest me!"

The police ignored her.

"Ma'am…"

"Don't ma'am me, young man. I'm not that old."

"And furthermore…" Aunt Frances was lecturing the police chief, who looked like he was one irate senior citizen away from a heart attack for Christmas.

The older man strode over to the holding cell, coffee mug in hand, teeth gritted. "I believe it's absurd how much of my tax dollars were spent on the new motorcycles. I saw Winston here crash his into a snowdrift, and I use the word *crash* liberally. It's more like he slowly drifted off course, and the bike fell."

The chief sucked in a breath and bellowed, "All of you need to get the fuck out of here!"

The rest of the townspeople scattered.

I narrowed my eyes. "Where is the district attorney? Are you pressing charges?"

The chief looked around and sighed. "We can keep her here, by law, for twenty-four hours."

"No, you're not keeping my client here for twenty-four hours!" I barked. "This jail does not meet the minimum standards for a holding cell under the new law passed this legislative session. You need to bring it up to compliance if you're keeping anyone here."

The drunk across from Emmie heaved himself up. "S'tha means I c'leave?"

"No," the chief snapped. "Your sister said to leave you here to sober up." He turned on me. "I don't need some big shot city lawyer coming into my town, telling me how to run my precinct. This is the way we've done things for a hundred years. I ain't changing now." The chief paused, pushed up his glasses, and peered at me. Then he made a noise of disgust. "Oh, you're Randall's boy. Shoulda known."

It didn't matter that I was in my thirties—I'd always live in my father's shadow here, it seemed.

"So is the DA pressing charges or not?" I asked.

"The DA's having a working lunch."

"Translation, the DA is out drinking on the city's dime. Fantastic. I will be taking my client, then, since no charges are being filed."

"I'm here! I'm here!" An older man in suspenders, a bow tie, and round spectacles hurried into the room, reeking of cigar smoke and whiskey.

"You called me here for Brucey? Brucey, what did we tell you? You can drink in public, but you can't be a nuisance," the DA scolded the drunk.

"No, it's the murderer." The chief pointed with his coffee mug.

"A murder?" The DA flailed. "Here in Harrogate? Someone call the National Guard—there's a murderer loose!"

"She's not loose. We have her."

"Sir," I began.

"Oh, you're Randall's boy!" The DA beamed at me. "How's he doing in retirement?"

"He and my mom are in the French Riviera, enjoying themselves."

"Wonderful!"

"Wouldn't catch me dead in France," the police chief said mulishly.

"My client—"

"Brucey?"

"Emmie Dawson," her grandmother sobbed. "You locked up my granddaughter."

"Surely there's been some mistake!" the DA exclaimed. "Pretty girl like that."

The police chief rolled his eyes

"I'm glad you and I see eye to eye." I shook the DA's hand.

The police chief threw down his papers.

"You do not have enough evidence to keep Ms. Dawson," I argued. "We don't know if those are even her cupcakes. Someone could have made cupcakes that looked like hers and poisoned them."

Emmie hiccupped. "But they look just like my cupcakes. It's a custom design."

"Ms. Dawson, please shut up, and please let me handle this. Unless you do want to go to prison."

"She can and should be in prison!" Theo blustered.

Yes, Theo, the man who'd bought my father's legal practice because I was a terrible son and refused to come home to Harrogate to run it.

I hated him.

I pulled myself up to my full height, still pettily happy I was taller than him.

I am not a teenager or some snot-nosed twentysome-thing recent grad. I should not care. It's unreasonable to care. Theo is nothing.

"Why are you releasing her?" Theo still had that same whiny nasal voice.

"Because my client is innocent," I snapped.

"She killed my best friend; she killed Brooks. Justice for Brooks! The man had a baby on the way."

"Theo, my boy!" The DA and Theo embraced.

"We still doing drinks tonight?" Theo asked.

"Don't I know it? My treat," the DA said.

None of this would fly in NYC.

I felt the annoyance rise and tried to lower my hackles. This was why I'd left Harrogate—this petty small-town bullshit.

"Emmie murdered Brooks. Everyone saw it. There are a hundred witnesses," Theo argued.

The DA squirmed.

"She didn't. There were no witnesses. Just because Ms. Dawson was in the vicinity doesn't mean she had anything to do with his death. We don't even know if it was the cupcakes," I argued. "He could have had a burst appendix. He could have had an allergic reaction. It could have been anything. You might as well arrest everyone who was in the café this morning."

"He does have a point..." Emmie made big teary eyes at the DA.

"That girl can't sit in a jail cell. Chief, let her out." The DA motioned.

The chief's keys jangled.

"You're not going anywhere, are you, Ms. Emmie?" the DA asked.

"No, she is not a flight risk," I assured him before Emmie could say something stupid.

I grabbed her arm and half dragged her back out into the cloudy winter afternoon.

She shivered on the sidewalk.

"You got me out of jail." She seemed to be in shock.

Begrudgingly, because I knew my mother would materialize from France just to yell at me, I wordlessly took off my coat and draped it around her.

"Thank you." The young woman clutched at the coat. "I can't believe you were able to get me out of jail." She stared up at me in a daze.

"Just for today," I warned.

"Just today?"

"They could still arrest you, for keeps this time."

The tears started again. Moose wound around her feet.

Emmie's grandmother was there to envelop her in a warm hug as the seniors cheered.

"You did it!" My aunt kissed my cheek. "You saved the day!"

"Aunt Frances, that is not how this works. There will be a trial. In fact, I would bet anything that Theo will convince the DA to do so at their next little drink session."

Aunt Frances nudged me as Emmie sobbed on her grandmother's shoulder. "So you're taking her case?"

I reminded myself no good deed went unpunished. I shouldn't get any more involved. Small-town girl's hubby was cheating on her. She axed him. The end.

But what if she didn't?

And if not, then who did?

"She's cute," Aunt Frances whispered. "Women fall in love with their saviors, you know!"

"Yes, I am taking her case, but I'm not getting romantically involved with a person who allegedly poisoned her husband."

"You're a man with a cat on a leash," my aunt said flatly. "Your options are limited."

CHAPTER 3
Emmie

E ven though the great room of the retirement community was warm, with a big fire in the oversize stone fireplace, I was shivering.

"I'm sorry, Gran," I whispered as the police officers carted boxes of "evidence" out of Granny Edna's flat. "I should never have moved in here. I should have moved in with Zoe."

"Yeah." Gran nodded. "She's dating one of them Svensson brothers. They give money to the police. They would never have gotten their house searched. Hey! You get your hands off that dildo. That was a gift." She raced after one horrified officer, who promptly dropped the box and ran, almost bowling over Cora, who sidestepped him, carrying a box of food for her daily visit with her grandmother.

Abbott from the newspaper snuck in behind Cora. I didn't have the energy to chase away the reporter. I closed my eyes and leaned my throbbing head back against the couch armrest.

I was stuck in a nightmare.

I'd always secretly hoped Brooks would get what was coming to him—that karma would kick him in the teeth—but murder?

Maybe it was just an allergic reaction.

He was my husband—had been for years. He didn't have any allergies.

Sometimes people can develop them late in life, I tried to assure myself.

I was so nauseous.

The only bright spot was Marius rescuing me out of that smelly, frigid jail cell.

Now he was talking with the police detective. I gazed at him.

The suit, the height, the brown hair with the crisp part—he was every part the big New York City lawyer.

Meanwhile, I was covered in cat hair and cupcake frosting.

"Oh, Emmie!"

Porcelain clattered as Cora set a steaming cup of tea down on the side table next to me.

"I brought cupcakes, but…" She looked anxiously over at the cops, who were finishing up their evidence collection.

"I need to wash all my clothes… vacuum." The task weighed heavily on my chest. My shoulders ached.

"You should eat something first," Cora fussed. "All the seniors are worried about you. I brought some perogies for the holiday snack table. You should have some."

"Thank you, but I'm not even hungry. Who knew your worthless husband dropping dead in your café would kick-start that New Year's diet?"

"They're good, though!" Ava called from the snack table laden with holiday treats. She added a cupcake to her plate. Then her eyes widened. "Er... you didn't make these, right, Emmie?"

I shook my pounding head. The room spun.

"Have some tea," Cora murmured.

"Have a cold soda instead." Abbott sat down on the couch next to me, jostling the teacup. He fanned himself. "Why do old people always need the room so hot?"

"Cora, I think your grandmother was looking for you!" Ava called. "Ida's selling inflatable sex dolls, and she wants you to unlock her credit card so she can buy one."

"Oh my God," Cora muttered, hurrying away.

My stomach roiled when I saw the reporter had a wilting cupcake on a plate.

He took a messy bite.

"So," the reporter said, chewing noisily, frosting dropping onto his wrinkled sports coat. "How much money did you make off of killing your husband?"

"*Make money?*" I screeched.

Abbott flinched, smearing the cupcake frosting on his mouth.

"You think I made money?" The tears were back. "You know, when he left me, he cleaned out the accounts. Everything. I lost everything. He kicked me out of my own house. I didn't make any money off of Brooks because he didn't have any money."

"Ah, so you killed him because you wanted to get even."

More frosting smeared as Abbott scribbled on the notepad.

"No, that's not—"

"Cross that out. That's not on the record. My client is not speaking with the press."

Abbott jumped with a squeak.

A shadow fell over us.

"Do, ah, do you have a statement?" the reporter asked.

"No comment."

Marius didn't step back. He just stood there, crowding me and Abbott, until the reporter got the hint and slid sideways off the couch and around the taller man. With a "Bye, Marius," he raced to the front door, grabbing another cupcake on the way out.

Marius leaned over me, resting one hand on the back of the couch. "What the hell are you doing, talking to the press? Maybe I should have just left you in jail."

"No, thank you." My chin quivered. I had sworn, after Brooks left me, that I wasn't crying over him or any man ever again, yet here I was.

"Really? Because I cannot think of another way to impress upon you the gravity of your situation. There are police crawling all over your grandmother's apartment, the town is calling for your head. All the circumstantial evidence and five thousand years of human history shows that you're the one who killed Brooks," he snarled, his deep voice a low rumble so only I could hear it. "Yet here you are, drinking tea and running your mouth to reporters. If you cannot cooperate, I'm going to leave you out to hang."

I gulped, trying to avoid his hazel eyes.

"Sorry," I said. "Sorry, I'm just—"

"Don't apologize to me." He stood up, smoothing his tie. "It's your life you're ruining."

"And all my cats' lives." The waterworks started again. Marius gave a long-suffering sigh.

"She's not bringing all those cats here, is she, Edna?" Cora's grandmother demanded.

"Lord, no," Granny Edna said, fanning herself.

"Can we turn up the heat in here, Edna?" The old woman scowled.

"If you did more than watch HGTV all day, maybe you'd handle the cold a little better, crotchety old hag."

"I'm so sorry I didn't come sooner." Zoe, my best friend since we were kids, rushed over to me through the lobby crowded with a house party of seniors watching my life fall apart. "Girl Meets Fig was crazy. Come on!" Zoe tugged me up. "Wash your face off. You can't just sit around here. It's not healthy."

"I guess I should go feed the cats."

"You need to stay away from the crime scene," Marius warned.

"Are *you* going to feed the cats?" Zoe pinned him with a withering glare. With Zoe's punk rock style and green hair for the holiday season, no one messed with her.

My friend adjusted her glasses. "Didn't think so. Let's go."

"So, props to you," Zoe said as we walked to my shop. It was late in the day and the winter sky, darkening.

"I didn't do it."

"You can tell me. I'm your bestie."

"I swear," I said. "No one believes me."

Zoe sighed. "Maybe I was just hoping you finally grew a pair for Christmas. Bastard had it coming, if you ask me."

"Who could have killed him?" I wondered anxiously.

"You can't tell me you're sad about that hemorrhoid."

"No. I mean, I don't know. We were married," I said, pulling out my keys to go in the back way, since the front entry was wrapped in crime scene tape.

In the dark alley, there was a crash of garbage cans.

"What the hell was that?" Zoe hissed, grabbing me.

There was rustling, then a black figure raced down the alley, away from my building.

"I bet that was the killer. We need to chase them," Zoe urged.

"No," I hissed, dragging her into the shop. It was unlocked.

I'm sure I locked it.

"I'm not running anywhere. We should just call the police. They'll see that I'm not the real killer, and this will all go away."

The 911 operator sounded annoyed when I called about the break-in. "Probably just someone wanting to see the crime scene for themselves. The killer doesn't return to the scene of the crime. This isn't a movie." The operator hung up.

"Maybe it's an inside job," Zoe said as I opened the door.

"Hi, babies!" I cooed to the cats that wound around my legs.

"This is a lot of cats," Zoe said slowly, kicking the snow off her heavy black boots.

"Oh," I said as all the yellow eyes stared at me in the dark. "I guess you don't realize how many there are when the café is busy." I bit back a sob.

"Don't cry. Even if you might potentially be going to prison, it's worth it now that bastard Brooks is dead. Not to mention you get all the money."

"There is no money."

Zoe raised an eyebrow. "There is always money. Somewhere."

I started scooping cat food into the bowls, and Zoe distributed them around the kitchen.

"I'm not supposed to feed them in here, but now that does it matter," I said sadly. "It's all over. The death of the dream. This was all I had. I took out a loan for this café. I'm never going to pay it back. I'm going to go bankrupt." I sounded hysterical. "This was all I ever wanted. I thought when Brooks left me that at least I could open up a café like I'd always dreamed of. Brooks always told me I would fail. He was right."

"Don't let that asshole ruin this for you from beyond the grave." Zoe shook my shoulders roughly. "I'm about ready to book you a séance with Lilith so she can tell him to go to hell."

I gazed mournfully at the cupcakes, frosting peaks tall and stiff since they were the green-and-red Grinch cupcakes with the Grinch Mountain in frosting. They'd never go out in the advent calendar.

I should have swept the cupcakes into the trash, but I couldn't bear to throw away my hard work.

"It's too bad they won't let you reopen," Zoe said, picking up one of the Grinch cupcakes and peeling off the paper wrapper. "Girl Meets Fig was doing a ton of business

just because we're down the street from the murder café."
She opened her mouth to take a bite.

"No!" I screamed. "Don't eat that!"

Zoe gave me an odd look. "Did you actually poison him, Emmie?" she asked, peering at me in the dim light from the stove light. "I mean no shade. Props to you, just..."

"No," I said. "I'm not like you. I'm weak. I could never. I couldn't even leave Brooks years ago when I really should have. It's just... What if the murderer poisoned all my cupcakes?"

"Tastes fine to me," Zoe said, chewing. "You need to find a way to reopen immediately and take advantage of being the murder café. I bet you pay back your loan in, like, a week."

"How? I can't. I need to concentrate on staying out of jail."

Zoe smirked. "You could ask your hot lawyer."

"He's not—"

"Hot? Uh, yeah, he is. And I say this as someone happily in a relationship. Dude is fine as hell. That suit? Chef's kiss. And you know I am not one for a man in a suit."

"Okay, fine, he's cute," I grumbled.

"Fine," Zoe corrected. "Fuh-*ine*. With two syllables. The way he was standing over you? No wonder it was so hot in that room."

"I can't ask him for help."

"Why not? I bet he can snap his fingers and have this place open."

"I—I don't know." I rubbed my arm.

"You need to be more assertive. You're a small-business owner and a mom to twenty-five-ish," Zoe said as the cats all meowed in a mass around the food. "You're a grown-up. You can ask for what you need. The worst he can say is no."

"But I'm not paying him."

"This is a small town. Barter and beg, baby!"

I should have worn something a little more attractive that wasn't covered in cat hair if I was going to go beg Marius for help.

Especially since he looked like that.

I froze in the dark archway to the empty great room later that evening after playing with the cats and getting a pep talk from Zoe.

With one leg bent and the other outstretched, he was like a Victorian portrait in the wingback chair. His Bengal cat snoozed on the rug in front of the fire. He'd opened the windows, and the fresh winter air blew in, relieving the room of its stuffy heat.

The tall man was reading through legal papers written in tiny font, marking things with a red pen, and jotting down notes on a legal pad in a leather portfolio.

I shouldn't interrupt him—it was a weekday. The man obviously had a real job that wasn't helping me with problems caused by my terrible decisions.

But…

Zoe would yell at me if I didn't at least try.

I squared my shoulders and marched into the great room before I could chicken out.

"I-I just," I stammered, "forgot my book."

Marius looked up, his hazel eyes almost gold in the firelight. "I didn't see one." He frowned.

I panicked. "Maybe the police took it."

He set down his pen. "We need to talk about your case."

"You don't want to get more comfortable?"

The raising of his eyebrow let me know that comment might have been a little bit forward.

I chewed on my lip. "I didn't mean it like that."

"Too bad. I enjoy it when my clients proposition me in exchange for free work."

"Oh well..." I was flustered. "I mean, I suppose you can't be expected to work for free."

"Seriously," he said dryly. "I'm not going to sleep with you. I'd be disbarred." He turned back to his paperwork, dismissing me. "Come find me tomorrow when you're ready to be rational."

His derision stuck in the back of my throat. I was done with men treating me like I was some weak little girl.

"So I think I have a lead on the case." I stepped in front of him.

He made an annoyed sound. "We'll speak tomorrow when you've had a chance to calm down."

"I *am* calm. I can also pay you," I said, taking out my wallet. "I respect your time and want to compensate you. I don't need any favors."

Marius looked up, incredulous. "You can't afford me."

"Yes, I can." I was stubborn. "What's your rate?"

"It's eight hundred dollars an hour."

"Oh." I deflated.

"I charge in six-minute increments," he added.

"Well, I can get a public defender. I know you have a real job."

"Ms. Dawson, you will not get a public defender."

"Why not?"

"Because," he said, "my aunt will kill me if I back out. I owe her. She put me through law school and bought me a two-bedroom apartment in Manhattan—well, it was her husband's money, but still. Like your ex, he also managed to die before he could divorce my aunt for his mistress. But now you're the hottest widow in Harrogate."

I was indignant. "You can't believe I'm the killer."

"Of course I think you're the killer," he scoffed.

"Then why are you helping me?" I cried.

"Because my aunt guilt-tripped me. Not because I like you. Certainly not because I think you're innocent." He turned back to his papers. "Don't worry. I'll put you under the pro bono hours. It's just a matter of filing some paperwork."

"I don't want you to do something you're not comfortable with," I snapped, "since apparently, the last man I was legally tied to decided he needed to *die* to get away from me."

Marius was suddenly still, pinning me with his courtroom gaze. He stood up slowly, his face in shadow from the fire. "You didn't actually kill him, right?" The deep voice dropped an octave, making me shiver.

"Of course not."

With a sharp jerk of his hand, he flicked his pen onto the couch and advanced on me.

I scuttled back until my hip banged the corner of the sideboard. He was right up on me, backing me up against the wall, staring into my eyes.

"Do not lie to your lawyer." He leaned in. "I'm going to ask you again. Did you kill Brooks, Ms. Dawson?"

I shook my head. "No, I didn't kill him. I swear."

Marius stared at me for several excruciating moments then mercifully stepped back.

"It is really, really warm in here." I gasped for breath.

"Maybe you should take off all that flannel." The corner of his mouth quirked. He turned around.

Was he flirting with me? More likely, he was teasing me about my awkward statement.

No way would I want to be with him. He's a prick, I decided as I climbed up the stairs to my grandmother's apartment.

To avoid thinking about Marius, I considered the unlocked door and the person running from my café.

It wasn't a tourist. It had to be someone involved in the murder. That was the only logical explanation—they were removing evidence.

The police were trying to gaslight me, but I was going to solve the mystery.

I logged into the web server for the cheap security camera I'd stuck with double-sided tape on the brick alley wall. It wasn't anything like the fancy ones and only took a photo when there was motion, but there was a blurry black-and-white image on my screen.

"I knew I didn't kill my husband!" Now everyone else was going to know it too. "And Marius is going to help me—bad attitude or not."

CHAPTER 4
Marius

The only good thing about spending December with Aunt Frances was this. Breakfast.

She lived in a very expensive senior living center. I knew. I paid the bill every month. And it came with catered breakfast and lunch.

"I'm not giving you any," I warned the cat. "You already ate."

Moose meowed for some of the sausage patty smothered in gravy.

"You want to turn that OJ into a mimosa?" asked Sadie, who owned the Southern-inspired catering company.

"I have to work. I'm reviewing that contract for your husband's company," I reminded her.

Over in the corner, her husband, Parker Svensson—yeah, those Svenssons—was standing around, scowling.

"I told him he didn't need to come. He refused, what with the murderer loose." Sadie gave me a pointed look.

"I'm not discussing my clients," I reminded her.

"Boo. There's lots more gravy—don't be shy!"

I dug into the hashbrowns and cheesy scrambled eggs. I'd gone for a run in the snowy morning but probably hadn't done enough to justify getting a second plate.

"Our first suspect." A printout of a blurry photo was shoved in front of me right when I was about to take a bite of the fresh steaming biscuit.

"Ms. Dawson—"

"Emmie," she said determinedly. "We're going to be spending a lot of time together."

"No, we're not."

"We have to investigate the case, and this," she said, tapping the photo with her fork, "is suspect number one."

"Who is it?" I tried to hand the photo back to her.

She ignored it in favor of taking a big bite of her breakfast. "I don't know. That's what we're going to investigate."

"You're not a detective."

"You don't know me."

"Well, for once, you're not drinking with breakfast. I'm surprised you didn't get a mimosa."

"I didn't know we could have mimosas." Emmie looked around.

Sadie came over with a bottle and splashed a generous amount into her glass. It had a strong chemical smell.

"Wait. I thought that was window cleaner," I said slowly. Sadie blinked.

Emmie took a sip of her orange juice mixed with kerosene.

"That's what we sell it as to avoid the alcohol tax, but everyone who's in the know knows." Emmie tapped her head.

A few tables away, a senior citizen was using the moonshine to light up one of those spinning candle decorations.

"How the fuck am I here for a month?" I asked myself.

The smell of the alcoholic orange juice wafted over to me.

Revolting.

"So, my case. This suspect was in my shop."

"Yes, we need to talk about the case," I interrupted her smoothly.

"We are…"

"No. One, you need to stay away from the crime scene, full stop."

"But—"

"Two, as your lawyer, I highly recommend you hire a different lawyer."

"But last night, you said…" The tears started, then she seemed to fight them back.

So she had a backbone after all.

"This is going to be a long case for you," I explained. "These criminal cases drag on for years. I'm going back to New York City after Christmas. You need someone local."

"No, I need you as my lawyer. And we're going to solve the case before Christmas. I can't have being a murder suspect hanging over my head for the holidays. That will ruin Christmas," Emmie said determinedly.

"If wishful thinking got innocent pleas, no one would be in jail," I said flatly.

"But you got me out of prison. You're a miracle worker."

"For now," I repeated. "When Theo"—I bit back the curse I usually added to his name—"has had enough drinks with the DA, he's going to have a judge sign a warrant for your arrest. Guaranteed."

"Yeah, but—"

"They're going to send it out to the county, and they're going to pin it on you. It's an election year. The mayor is going to want this case wrapped up. You're the prime suspect in this. You need someone who knows the judges and can get you a good plea deal."

"I'm innocent!" she cried.

"Up to a jury to decide."

"There aren't any other lawyers. The other lawyer in town is Brooks's friend Theo. He's *awful*." She spat out the word.

I immediately tensed and fought down the possessive urge to grab her and demand she tell me what he'd done to her.

You don't care about her. Or him.

The last time I was here, I'd gone into a death spiral, ruminating over how terrible Theo and Brooks had been to me.

I'd even bought a voodoo doll yesterday morning to sooth my inner child.

We are better than this.

"I need my shop open. The cats. My money. Oakley is in my house," she begged.

"Don't start throwing her out," I warned, taking another sip of my coffee. "You don't want to get a fine for illegal eviction."

"Brooks probably gave her the house in the will anyway," she said bitterly. "He ruined everything. I wish I'd never met Brooks."

Same.

I wiped my mouth. "Hurry up and finish eating," I ordered. "I'm going to get your shop back."

The Santa Claws Café was the legal definition of a shit show.

Police and crime scene techs were moseying around, talking nonsense and pretending they were in the holiday special of *Law and Order*.

"I've been at crime scenes for mass murders in New York City that had less police activity than this cupcake shop." I handed Moose to Emmie and stepped into the café. "Excuse me."

They look up at me. One of the cops beamed. "Marius! Look who's back in town."

"You literally saw me over Thanksgiving," I reminded Bobby.

"Good to see a familiar face." He rocked on his heels.

He and I had joined forces in middle school on more than one occasion. Safety in numbers from Brooks and his thuggish friends and all.

"Ms. Dawson needs the use of her cupcake shop. You all were here all day yesterday. You don't need to gather any more evidence."

One of the crime-scene techs swallowed the cupcake he was eating.

"Are you going to pay for that?" I demanded.

"It's on the house!" Emmie called. "Did you like it? I added cardamom."

"It's delicious!" The crime scene tech flashed a thumbs-up.

"Have another."

"No. They need to vacate the shop. You are all violating Ms. Dawson's fourth amendment rights."

"You mean the right not to have the British move into your house?" Officer Girthman frowned.

"No. It's a taking. Unreasonable search and seizure. You already searched Ms. Dawson's shop. You can't also keep it closed indefinitely. Are you charging her?" I demanded. "Well?"

The police bumbled around.

"I guess we have enough evidence. You can open your shop, Emmie," Winston said, taking down the crime scene tape.

When they finally left, plied with cupcakes I wouldn't eat, considering they came from Santa's little murder bakery, Emmie threw herself into my arms.

It was startling, the softness of her.

"Thank you," she whispered. "You're my hero."

It took me a minute to gather my wits enough to say, "No, I'm not."

CHAPTER 5

Emmie

"**B**ack in business." I sighed.

I'd cleaned up the café and assured the cats that everything was back to normal, and no, Moose wasn't going to stay and eat the food, but they did need to be nice and let him use the litter box, considering his cat daddy had saved us all.

I snuck a glance at Marius.

The tall man was leaning against the counter, arms crossed like those hot lawyers in the sitcoms on cable TV Gran liked to watch. He had that self-assured carelessness well-to-do men had.

Moose leaped up to Marius's massive shoulders while he typed on his phone with one hand, sipping a coffee held in the other.

Someone had posted that the Santa Claws Café was open for business again, and the customers were starting to stream in, though there was a lot more gawking than buying.

"Cat daddy is right."

"Shhh!" I hissed at Zoe as I packaged up the cakes for Girl Meets Fig.

"He clearly likes you a little bit, or he'd have gone off to sign things, yell at people, or whatever it is lawyers do when they aren't in court, not stand guard in your shop."

The police chief stuck his head inside, Theo hot on his heels.

"This café cannot be allowed to be in business." Theo was steaming. "It's a site of a horrific crime against humanity."

The police chief walked up to Marius.

Marius gave him a coldly professional smile. "As I informed the last two officers who came in here to harass my client, the City of Harrogate cannot legally keep this café closed indefinitely. There were no health department violations logged, and Ms. Dawson has paid her taxes and licensing fees. She has gone over and above to cooperate with the investigation of the death of Brooks Dawson. However, now it has become egregious. She will not be cooperating any further in what is turning into a witch hunt to cover up shoddy police work."

The police chief just sighed loudly and shook his head while Theo sputtered.

"Don't just let him steamroll you."

"I did clerk with one of the current Supreme Court justices, and I am prepared to take this case all the way to the top if need be," Marius added.

"Threats! I will get a warrant for Emmie's arrest. Murderer!" Theo yelled at me.

"Slander! We're suing, right, Marius?" Zoe shouted.

Marius ignored my friend.

"Fine. Fuck it." Zoe rolled up her sleeves.

Theo took an apprehensive step backward.

"I'll beat your ass in the middle of Main Street, boy."

"You don't work for the city, Theo. You're not the DA," Marius said in a clipped tone. The words were professional, but the tone said *fuck off*. "You're not getting a warrant. Now, I must ask you to leave. Ms. Dawson does not consent to you being on her property, and any further trespassing will be considered unlawful, and I will formally lodge a complaint."

I had to hold Zoe back.

Marius watched like a predator as my deceased husband's best friend and the annoyed police chief left. Then he settled and went back to his phone, still keeping one watchful eye on the door.

"He's like a dressed-up high-end guard dog," Zoe marveled.

"Ms. Dawson does not have any comments about recent events!" he barked before Abbott could race up to me, microphone out for a statement. "Purchase something, or get out."

Abbott looked apprehensively at the cupcakes behind the glass case.

Zoe took a big bite. "Yum! Tastes amazing."

"I guess I'll take two."

After I packaged up his purchase, Gran hustled out of the kitchen, where she and several of her friends were helping me restock my cupcake supplies. The cupcake advent calendar was a day behind, and I needed a thousand peppermint-bark cupcakes yesterday.

"You need to give that man a blowjob. We're about to go on break," she hissed at me too loudly. I saw the muscle in Marius's cheek twitch. "Just take him to the storeroom. You're almost out of flour, by the way."

I turned my back to Marius. "I'm not—no!"

"He's doing all sorts of free labor for you," Gran argued. "He's done more for you in twenty-four hours than Brooks ever did, and you were shackled to that walking prolapsed anus for seven years."

I gave Marius a guilty glance. He *was* doing a lot. Just heading off the prying questions and dissuading the police from shutting down my shop was keeping my mental state from driving off a cliff.

I went into the kitchen, dodging seniors running around with vats of batter and huge bags of frosting, and put together a selection of snacks for him. Plate and fresh cup of coffee in hand, I approached Marius.

"I know this isn't a drop in the bucket to repay you," I said, "but I thought you might need some sustenance."

He peered down his nose at the plate.

"Murder cupcakes? No, thank you."

I slammed the plate down on the counter next to him. "Fine," I spat. "Do you want a blow job instead?"

"No man wants to get involved with a sheltered small-town widow—married young to a piss-poor excuse for a man, too stupid to move out of town, and too useless to get a real job," he drawled. "Now, if you were a divorcée, I'd know that at least the sex would be wild before you eventually offed me for the money."

"You think I'm dumb?" I couldn't stop the tears. Fuck him.

"Please stop crying. You know it's true. You married Brooks, after all. I'm sure all of your friends told you not to."

I cried harder because they had. Zoe had staged an intervention.

But I had been in *love*.

"I know I should never have married him, but I didn't kill him." I wiped my face, trying to get ahold of myself. "We need to solve the mystery."

"*You* need to," he corrected. "Otherwise, you're going to prison."

"You're not helping?"

"This isn't the movies; lawyers don't investigate crimes. We make sure that the proper legal proceedings have been followed. Come Christmas, I'm out of here," he warned.

"I know. I'm working on it. I have a suspect."

"You have half a suspect." He nodded as Charles came in, irate. "Now, him? That's a suspect. Could he have murdered Brooks and now, succumbing to guilt, returned to the scene of the crime?"

"Marius, don't." I grabbed his arm, which was surprisingly muscular under the suit. Probably all he did was work out and act like an asshole to people.

Too late. Charles had heard Marius, and his anger had ratcheted up to fury.

"Well, well, well. If it isn't a Christmas miracle. Santa's little cupcake shop of horrors open for business," Charles sneered.

Outside, Gertrude, Alice, and several other members of the feral-cat committee were gearing up for a protest. It was shaping up to be a headache-inducing day.

Ducking behind the counter, I ate a chocolate cherry cupcake with red-star sprinkles.

"You do all realize," Charles said loudly to my customers, "that you are consuming cupcakes laced with poison."

I stood up, almost banging my head on the underside of the counter, and wiped crumbs off my mouth. "Aren't you going to sure him for slander?" I asked Marius.

"It's not slander if it's true!" Charles thundered. "You're a mean one, Emmie. You're stealing business from me. Your cats are a menace to Main Street. My sales are down thirty percent because of you. You ruin lives for profit. You are more than capable of killing your husband."

"You could have easily killed him yourself," Zoe shot back. "You never liked Emmie's shop. I bet you killed him to frame her. Murderer!"

Abbott scribbled the accusations furiously on his notepad.

"You give me that!" Charles raged, chasing him out of the shop, almost bowling over Cora, who walked in confused.

"I have a delivery for…" Cora looked around, frowning. "Marius? This is awkward."

"Thank you. I'll take that." Marius accepted the food from Cora and handed her a crisp twenty.

"*You're buying food from next door?*" I screeched as he unwrapped the sandwich.

He nodded silently toward the feral-cat committee, who chanted, "Cats and murder go hand in hand, like Christmas in summer or snow in the sand!"

"You need to get a restraining order," Zoe said as she headed to the door with her boxes for Girl Meets Fig.

"Here's your mail, Emmie," Cora said sheepishly.

Muttering "Thanks," I took the mail back to the kitchen storeroom, away from the nosy customers, the well-meaning seniors, the accusations of murder, and Marius and his stupid handsome face.

"Asshole," I cursed then ripped open my advent calendar, stuffed the last two days' worth of chocolate into my mouth, and chewed furiously. Then I tore open the rest of the doors.

I hadn't slept the night before, just tossed and turned on the couch.

I sank down onto the cold tile floor, trying not to hyperventilate.

I was going to be fine. The shop was going to be fine. Everything would be *fine*.

I peered at something sparkling under the shelf. After tossing aside the half-empty advent calendar, I reached under and scooped with my pen until I dragged out a thin sparkling silver bracelet—simple and elegant with a stunning emerald and ruby.

A clue.

This was what the suspect had been looking for last night. I was sure of it.

CHAPTER 6
Marius

"You don't have to come." Emmie was stubborn as we walked through the dark street toward city hall.

"I wasted all day at your café," I reminded her. "It would be just my luck that you'd do something incriminating when left to your own devices, then I'd have to hear about it from Aunt Frances, who would expect me to pull miracles."

"You are impressive," Emmie said begrudgingly. "You just have a caustic personality."

"Because I'm dealing with a child who wants to end up back in jail. Now, as your lawyer…" I stepped in front of Emmie. She slid on the icy concrete. I grabbed her before she could knock into me. "I would advise you not to attend this meeting."

"I'm the social chair of the feral-cat committee," she said, jaw set. "I don't miss meetings."

Why I'd thought it would be any different when we stood in the doorway of the small meeting room in city hall, I didn't know.

Moose hissed from my shoulder as all of the cats in the room sprang onto the furniture, fought over bowls of food, and tried to escape into the hallway.

I rubbed my jaw.

I recognized Cora, who was a neighboring shop owner, and Alice and Gertrude from the protests.

"Hi, Rosie!" Emmie greeted a fourth woman.

"Order. *Order!*" Gertrude banged a cat-shaped gavel, causing several cats to scurry.

"Oooh! A new member! Don't worry," Rosie purred to me. "We don't bite. Except for David. He definitely snapped at a police officer the other day. Don't worry. As the new person earlier this year, I'll show you the ropes. You just stick with me, handsome."

I turned back to the meeting. The weirdo cat-committee people were now in a shouting match about proper fees for adopting a cat.

"I can barely give away a cat," Emmie was arguing. "We can't charge for them. They're stray animals!"

"That's why you murdered your husband!" Gertrude thundered. "To drum up business for your café. You are using these poor innocent cats for your own financial gain."

"Don't," Rosie whispered when I was about to interject. "They hate her." She ran her hand up and down my arm. "Gertrude and Alice were talking about it earlier."

Across the room, Emmie glared at me.

I smirked at her.

But my mind was racing.

Could it be that Emmie had been the real target all along, not Brooks? If so, she could be in danger.

"When you said 'widow'"—there was a twitch of a smile on Grayson's mouth—"I was thinking, you know, a widow. Not…"

Not Emmie with her too-tight sweaters, the apron that hugged her curves, and literal rosy cheeks.

"She looks like she should be on a Christmas card, greeting you with a homemade dinner and a baby on her hip." My friend and boss had just come into town with his girlfriend. Lexi was shopping. He was there under duress.

His two Dalmatians wagged their tails furiously as I petted their big sleek heads.

I buttoned up my coat and let the door shut behind me.

"Isn't that the cat girl who nerfed her cheating husband?" A group of excited teenagers stopped in front of the café, and I opened the door for them.

"Everyone's talking about it." I sighed.

"You're her lawyer." Grayson raised an eyebrow. "What do you mean, 'everyone'?"

I grimaced.

"Rookie mistake, letting the publicity go wild," I admitted. "Though it shouldn't be that big of a deal."

"The tabloids got ahold of it. She has means, motive, and opportunity. It's all over the internet, or so Lexi tells me," Grayson unhelpfully reminded me.

"You didn't want to spend time shopping with her?"

"Lexi says she didn't want to ruin my surprise Christmas present," he said dryly.

"I hope it's something noisy and colorful." I smirked as we headed into the lively Christmas market.

Everyone was capitalizing on the cupcake murder. Murder-related merchandise was everywhere. The food stalls even had murder-themed offerings.

I didn't live in Harrogate, but I was sure it wasn't normally this busy on a weekday. The cupcake murders had attracted a crowd. People were standing around, speculating about whether Emmie had done it.

"What do you think?" Grayson asked.

"It doesn't matter; she claims she's innocent, and as her lawyer, that's what I have to go with."

"It doesn't have anything to do with a pretty damsel in distress needing to be rescued?" His mouth twitched.

"I think I liked you better when you were anti love and relationships," I snipped.

Grayson just smirked.

"Besides, I only date other lawyers, not a literal widow with twenty cats. I need someone who understands me."

Moose, riding on the back of one of the Dalmatians, meowed at me.

"Don't want to be a stepfather?" Only someone who had known Grayson as long as I had would detect the undercurrent of humor. "Also didn't the last lawyer you dated dump you because her dad was mad you didn't go to Yale?"

"Maybe."

We walked in silence for a moment.

"Emmie Dawson doesn't seem like the murdering type," Grayson said.

"They never do."

We headed past a stall selling Christmas ornaments made out of beer cans.

"You don't think she did it?" Grayson asked after a moment.

"If it goes to trial, I could make a good case that it was someone else."

"Who?"

"Not sure yet. Small towns aren't like the city. People hold grudges. The motive could be as simple as someone said something mean to someone in high school, and they finally got revenge."

"Then you're suspect number one."

"Fuck off." I elbowed my friend.

There was a skit underway at the stage in the center of the market. The children were acting out the gruesome cupcake murder. One little boy took a large bite out of a cupcake then convulsed dramatically. Then the grim reaper solemnly came out and took him away. The kids linked hands and bowed to applause.

"What kind of wholesome small-town event is this?" Grayson hissed in my ear.

The grandmaster of the Christmas market blared into a megaphone, "Stay tuned for part two of the *Cupcake Murders* next week, folks. And now on to the raffle."

Grayson handed me a scrap of paper and shifted the dog leashes to his other hand. "I bought you a raffle ticket."

"Only tourists buy raffle tickets."

"Don't those people live here?" Grayson nodded. Oakley and Beatrice were close to the front of the crowd, giving flowers to the kids who had just finished the play, many of them little blond doppelgangers of their older, more obnoxious Svensson siblings.

"Don't let them see us," I hissed as the brothers collected the kids.

"Too late."

Garret, a blond man, locked in on us. He sneered, "Why aren't you at work? Don't you have a contract you're supposed to be finishing for us?"

One of his little brothers flung himself down to the ground and bit Garrett's shoe. "I didn't get a cupcake!"

"I just have to thank you and your brothers for putting this together, Garrett," Oakley said, sobbing, wearing a big black hat.

Beatrice handed her a handkerchief.

"It is so comforting in my time of need to see people care about Brooks's murder."

"My condolences for your loss," Grayson murmured.

"I have his child." Oakley rubbed her belly. "At least I have a piece of him left."

Garret picked up the screaming kid and yelled until the other kids stopped getting distracted by the lights and the townspeople and followed him.

"What kind of grieving girlfriend wants a gruesome play about the death of the father of her child?" Grayson asked me.

"Someone who is secretly glad he's dead, probably." I narrowed my eyes as I watched Oakley and Beatrice slowly make their way out of the Christmas market, causing as much commotion and drawing as much attention to their exit as they could.

"And for the raffle winner, number three hundred forty-five!"

"You won," Grayson said.

"Shut up," I hissed at him.

"Do we have a winner?" the grandmaster screamed, pointing at me. "Step right up and claim your prize!"

"You get it for me."

"I can't," Grayson said, clamping down the smile. "The dogs... You know how they are."

I trudged up the steps to shake hands and have my photo taken with my prize.

"You won!" Lexi screamed when I rejoined Grayson and the animals.

Grayson's girlfriend had shown up with a wheelbarrow—yes, a literal wheelbarrow—full of Christmas market crap like wreaths, ornaments, and disfigured-looking holiday decorations.

"I thought Grayson wasn't supposed to see his gift."

"I actually am having something custom-made," the short redhead sang. "It's going to be amazeballs! He's going to die when he sees it. Oops, wrong choice of words."

"I'll make sure Grayson practices his 'I love it' face," I joked with her.

"Oooh!" She looked down at the red-green-and-white-striped box in my hand. "No fair! You won murder cupcakes."

"I'm not eating them." I headed to a trash can.

Before the elf-shaped can could open its mouth, I was mobbed by the crowd.

"Fifty dollars! I'll give you fifty for those."

"A hundred or nothing!" Lexi yelled.

"How about a reindeer sausage," one guy offered. "Homemade?"

"Ooh, yes! Dinner tonight." Lexi accepted the cooler and added it to the pile on the wheelbarrow.

I watched, feeling like a third wheel as my best friend and the love of his life bickered good-naturedly over the amount of stuff she'd bought.

Grayson picked up the wheelbarrow handles.

"Going back to the hot widow?" Lexi waggled her eyebrows.

"Against my will."

"It's Christmas. Santa loves a good deed! Someone's at the top of the nice list!"

Emmie didn't notice me when I hovered in the back door to the kitchen, wanting to avoid the crush of gawkers in the shop.

Tongue poking between her lips, brow tense in concentration, she was using a syringe to squirt something into a set of cupcakes.

Though Oakley was acting suspicious and Charles and Gertrude and Alice all had motive to frame Emmie, I wasn't going to count her out.

She had access to not just her grandmother's medicine but that of all the elderly in the retirement community as well. Any one of those medications could have been deadly to Brooks.

I stepped back into the shadow of the alley and headed to the police station.

Of course, Winston gave me a blank look when I ask for the toxicology report.

He made a big show of shuffling the papers around. "I can't seem to find it."

In other words, they'd never had it done.

"Then I want a sample to do my own tests."

"I mean, Ida said it smelled like cyanide," Winston whined as he led me back to the evidence locker.

"Ida is old and crazy. What does she know?"

"Supposedly, that's how she killed her husband in the fifties. That's what my great-granny says anyways." He handed me one of the cupcakes in a bag.

I didn't take it. "What are you doing? You can't just hand it to me. There has to be a chain of custody."

I watched him as he filed a transfer request, and a courier showed up to take the sample to a lab I used in New York City.

"You're real good at this cop stuff," Winston said in admiration.

* * *

It was dark by the time I finally returned to the café.

My eyes adjusted to the dimness of the alley.

Why weren't there any lights back here?

Moose yowled as a cat knocked over a metal trash can.

Wait. Not a cat…

A dark figure raced by me out of the alley. I caught a whiff of almonds.

The hell?

So, Emmie's suspect was real after all.

The baker gave me a startled look when I opened the back door to the kitchen.

"I think I just saw your murderer."

CHAPTER 7
Emmie

As was fitting, it was dark and overcast as I tried to zip up my black funeral dress.

"The bus is leaving," Gran called.

"Can it wait?"

"Let's go. I want to get a good seat." Gran peered into the bathroom. "You need more shapewear."

"I'm already wearing two layers. Just help me with the zipper."

Gran gave a halfhearted tug on the zipper. It didn't budge. "You can wear one of my dresses."

One of the beaded monstrosities from the seventies? Wasn't this funeral going to be bad enough?

Outside, a horn blared.

"Don't leave without us!" Edna shouted.

I groaned as she hurried out the door.

I didn't have money to call a taxi. Though I didn't want to roll up at my husband's funeral in the senior bus, it was better than spending money I didn't have.

"Go up," I hissed, jumping up and down. The zipper inched up.

There was loud knocking on the front door. Gran must have locked herself out again.

"Coming! Can you just take down the cupcakes?" I yelled, running to the door in my stocking feet. "Oh!"

Marius drew back when he saw me standing there my dress half on.

"Emmie." He turned around abruptly.

The awkwardness hung in the air as I banged my elbow, trying to close the door. "I thought you'd already be there to get a good seat."

"Unlike the other residents of this building, I'm not particularly excited to attend the funeral."

I could hear the wry smile in the words.

"Really? Because you sound happy," I grumbled from the other side of the door, "or is that because you get to stand there in your suit and be superior?"

"Would you like some help?" he offered.

"Just tell the bus to wait for me."

"It's already left."

I raced to the window to see the bus driving off.

"Dammit." When I turned around, Marius was there.

"I'll give you a ride," he offered, motioning for me to turn.

My face hot for some reason—it was always so hot in the senior center—I turned my back to him. His fingers barely brushed my skin as he held the fabric together then tugged up the zipper.

I smoothed down the front of my dress and slipped on my heels.

Marius was already standing at the door, holding the dessert carrier and the casserole.

"Just a tip from your lawyer"—he bent down to murmur in my ear, making me shiver—"you might want to at least pretend to be sad."

Even though Brooks had been a cheating asshole, I wasn't going to show up to his funeral empty-handed. That was just not how I was raised.

I held the umbrella, sleet pattering the fabric, as Marius and I darted up to the house.

My house.

Where the funeral was being held.

Marius set the casserole and dessert on a groaning table laden with food.

Now that I was back in the house where Brooks and I had lived—mostly unhappily, though I'd tried to be a good wife—it hit me that he was well and truly gone. My marriage was done.

And I'd failed.

Oakley was wailing in front of the coffin.

Heart sinking, I approached, not sure if I wanted to see Brooks like this, all laid out.

Beatrice rushed over to her friend. "Oh, don't cry! Poor Oakley. Brooks is in a better place. He's smiling down on you and your beautiful baby."

Theo stood in the corner, fists clenched.

"We're going to say goodbye to Brooks," Beatrice said as Oakley sobbed.

Because of where I was standing, I was the only one who saw Beatrice lean over the coffin and snip a lock of Brooks's hair then tuck it into her pocket.

"Why don't we get you some food? You haven't had anything all day." Beatrice led Oakley away.

"Till death do us part." Zoe handed me a glass of wine and toasted me. "Congrats on escaping this wad of public restroom toilet paper."

"You won't believe what I just saw," I hissed, Marius's warning about looking sad completely forgotten.

"From a *corpse?*" Zoe almost shrieked when I told her what I'd seen. "She put it in her pocket?" Zoe made a face. "Maybe she's making some sort of unhinged memento for Oakley."

"No one can be that codependent in their friendship," I whispered behind my hand.

"You did have me check to see if you forgot a tampon up your snatch that one time, remember?"

"That's different. No one was dead."

"You monster!" Oakley screamed from the refreshment table. Then she was racing over to me, more like an angry rhino than a heavily pregnant woman.

I ran, keeping the chairs between us as Oakley charged me.

"You're taunting me and my baby!" she shrieked.

"In hindsight," I said to Zoe as I dodged the bouquet of flowers Oakley threw at me, "maybe bringing my usual sympathy cupcakes was the wrong idea."

I flinched as Oakley hurled a Santa's Surprise cupcake at me. It glanced off the wall, leaving a smear of red frosting on the white wallpaper I'd agonized over and Brooks had yelled at me about.

"She's taunting me. The murderer is taunting me. Emmie killed the love of my life, and now she's rubbing it in my face." Oakley's sobs were attracting the attention of the whole room.

"Beatrice." Marius was there. "Why don't we take Oakley outside? This isn't good for the baby."

"That's right—the baby," Oakley said, sinking dramatically into a chair.

"Why is Marius being nice to her?" Zoe hissed at me.

Yeah, why is he?

"Very suspicious. But not as suspicious as Beatrice..."

"It wouldn't surprise me in the least if Brooks was sleeping with multiple women." We glared after Beatrice and Oakley.

"And one of them got mad enough about it to kill him."

CHAPTER 8
Marius

I shouldn't have let the funeral get me so bent out of shape. I'd sworn I'd dance on Brooks's grave when he finally kicked the bucket. I just didn't know it would be so soon.

I'd listened, eating the plate of refreshments and making noncommittal noises while Zoe and Emmie excitedly told me their half-baked theories about Oakley or Beatrice being the killer.

It was possible. But if I was going to defend Emmie in court, I needed more than plausible deniability. We needed proof. Evidence, timeline, motive. The reading of the will would ideally provide that. But I hoped that it wouldn't just provide proof that Emmie had killed her husband.

She'd been shocked and Zoe, furious, when I'd played devil's advocate and suggested that maybe *Emmie* had been the one to find out about Beatrice and had killed Brooks.

Emmie had refused to ride back to the senior center with me, instead cramming into the bus and ignoring me all evening.

The next afternoon, I stepped into the dark alley. Emmie hadn't told me she'd seen any more evidence of the shadowy figure, so that was a probable dead end. It was likely a voyeur, though if I had to choose, I'd bet it was the crazy cat people who were camped out in front of the store. While Alice and Gertrude were still hell-bent on shutting the café down, Rosie seemed a little too interested in me, which was why I'd been entering the back way.

I reached for the door, preparing to knock.

Then I heard voices.

"Girl, you're going to get everything!" Zoe said, clapping her hands.

"Shh! We don't know that." That was Emmie hissing. "I bet Brooks fucked me over."

"I bet he was stringing Oakley along, especially if he and Beatrice had something going on." Zoe was excited.

"I mean, it would be nice to have the house back. And my car. And the life insurance cash," Emmie added, a smirk in her voice.

"Girl, you've been holding out…"

I backtracked, bracing for the cat protestors on Main Street so I could think.

Emmie did know about a life insurance policy, and it was likely a lot of cash. I'd have to make sure she didn't talk to anyone else about it.

Rosie blew me kisses as I walked past.

"Emmie," I said, approaching the counter.

She looked a little flustered.

"We have to go to the reading of the will now."

"Oh!" she exclaimed, feigning confusion. "Is it happening already? I can't imagine why I need to be there. Brooks will give everything to Oakley."

As I helped Emmie with her coat, Zoe flashed her a thumbs-up.

Emmie gave an imperceptible shake of her head.

"This is just like a movie," Emmie said as I hurried her along Main Street.

"Yeah. No one does will readings anymore unless you were rich or apparently lived in a kooky small town."

I held the door of my father's former office open for Emmie. The same shoe-repair store was on the bottom, the same carpet on the stairs as we climbed up to the wood-paneled state-of-the-art-in-the-1960s office. The only thing that had changed was Theo's name on the desk.

Somehow, the fact that nothing had been altered was more unnerving than if Theo had redone everything.

I hung up our coats on the worn coatrack and pulled out Emmie's chair for her in the conference room.

"I'll go fetch you a coffee, Oakley," Beatrice was saying as they entered behind us.

"I thought pregnant women couldn't have coffee," I said, staring at them.

"I meant decaf."

"She means tea," Beatrice said at the same time

Oakley glared at Beatrice. "Yes, some herbal tea."

Theo helped Oakley sit down, fussing over her, while Beatrice came back with a cup of steaming tea.

"Are you all right?" Theo asked her as he took a seat at the head of the table.

Oakley heaved a big sigh and took a noisy sip of her tea. "I will be as soon as I have the money I need to support the last piece of Brooks on this earth." The loud sobs started again. "I need to know my house is mine. I need to finish the nursery."

Emmie's face was dark. She stared straight ahead.

"Let's get on with it," Beatrice said with a strained smile. "Brooks would have wanted us—I mean you, Oakley—to be strong."

Theo shuffled papers. "As the executor of the will of Brooks Dawson, it is my duty in the State of New York to ensure his final wishes are carried out as specified in this legal document."

He cleared his throat and read:

"I, *Brooks Dawson*, being of sound mind and body, hereby declare this my last will and testament. To my beloved soon-to-be spouse, *Oakley*, I leave our family home, with all its belongings and memories, in gratitude for the years we spent together."

"What the fuck? He just changed the name on the will we wrote." Emmie was furious.

"If you can't mind your manners, you'll be thrown out," Theo sneered at Emmie.

My fingers dug into the leather seat.

Emmie's face was white.

"To my beloved Oakley, I also leave all of the jewelry, the car, the china, my art collection—"

I grabbed Emmie's hand before she could let out a swear word or five.

"Yes, oh my God, yes!" Oakley pumped a fist then realized it wasn't the best reaction to have and began to sob again. "Of course, I'd rather have Brooks than the money."

There was a knock on the door, and the paralegal entered.

"I'm in the middle of a will reading!" Theo barked.

"Yes," the paralegal said, wearing that blank face the really good paralegals had even though you knew they were dying inside. "But I found this stuck in the mail chute. I told you we needed to get that fixed. It pertains to the will."

"We just read the will," Oakley snapped at her. "It's *been read*. Now, give me my money."

Theo slowly unfolded the paper.

If I hadn't been there, I was sure that he would have just burned it up. His face went red as he read the revised copy of the will.

I stood up to read over his shoulder.

"Brooks has decided to give everything to his unborn child," I said. "Oakley's name is crossed out."

"No! It's a lie!" Oakley cried.

"It's signed and dated with Brooks's signature."

"Not a problem." Oakley patted her protruding belly.

"And should no child be born, then it reverts to the old will anyway, right?" Beatrice asked anxiously.

"Wrong," I said. "It goes to the legal next of kin, who would be Emmie."

"She's not kin."

"She's his spouse. She inherits his estate," I said.

Theo scowled.

"Guess you should have gone to an actual law school, not done an online degree." I couldn't help the dig, though I knew it was petty.

Theo glared murderously at me.

"I don't care. I'm going to have a big, beautiful baby." Oakley rubbed her belly.

"Oakley can't have the house," Emmie argued. "It's not Brooks's to give. That was our house."

"Your name is not on the deed," Theo said, pulling a document from the folder.

Tears pooled in her brown eyes. "Only because he said since I wasn't putting money for the down payment, I couldn't be on the deed. But then I ended up having to help him pay the mortgage. Now I know he didn't have any money because he was supporting his mistresses—"

"Mistresses?" Oakley snarled. "Brooks wasn't cheating on me."

Beatrice sat ramrod straight in her seat. Maybe Emmie and Zoe had been on to something at the funeral after all.

"So you paid rent, Emmie," Theo asked snidely.

"We'll contest it," I said to Emmie automatically. The last bit of estate law I'd done had been back at Harvard, but the thought of Brooks and Theo having the last word was intolerable.

"I want to contest the whole will! When was that will redone?" Emmie demanded, waving a folded stack of papers at Theo. "I have the latest will right here and the life insurance policy."

"Angry that you killed him for nothing?" Theo sneered.

"My client didn't—"

"Fuck you, Marius."

"Life insurance policy?" Oakley screeched. "That's mine!"

"Oh, he didn't have you change that," Emmie said sweetly, unfolding the paperwork and sliding it over. "Well, well. Guess he didn't love you that much after all. Shocking that the man you helped cheat would turn around and cheat you."

Beatrice made a strangled noise.

"At least I still have the car," Oakley snarled.

"Your child has the car," I corrected, "and furthermore, it's unclear if that baby is even Brooks's."

"How dare you!" Oakley jumped up.

"Before any property is transferred, we need to have confirmation of paternity." I stared at Theo, silently hoping he'd put up a fight just so I could wipe the floor with him in court. Petty? Yes. But holidays and small towns made people crazy.

"Fine," Theo spat, "we'll have confirmation."

"This is horrible!" Beatrice wailed.

"You'll have to wait until the baby is born," Oakley said. "I don't want to put little Brooks Jr. in danger. In the meantime, Theo, I want to sue her"—she pointed at Emmie—"for the life insurance money."

"I'll file the paperwork immediately."

"She killed him. I know she did." Emmie was fuming. "The will is proof! Brooks knew Oakley was up to something. That's why he changed the will. He didn't trust women. Ever. He always accused them of being gold diggers."

"It is suspicious," I agreed, "and it's good for you if this murder goes to trial. I have notes, and I had the paralegal make color copies of the will for my records."

"I want to sue," she demanded. "Right now!"

"You're not going to sue. You're going to go to your café and calm down."

"I'm not going to calm down." Emmie was hopping mad. "I'm going to *my house*."

CHAPTER 9

Emmie

My own house. I'd given that man tens of thousands of dollars, and he'd always hemmed and hawed about changing the deed.

Now it was too late.

The house was going to Oakley and her unborn child, Brooks Jr.

Now that the funeral was over, the big white Victorian house was decorated for Christmas.

"Those are my Christmas decorations!" I screeched. "I made half of those, and the rest are antiques. How *dare* she."

Inside, it was worse.

"How did Oakley do all this pregnant?" Marius frowned. "I remember when my mom was pregnant with my sister. She could barely move."

"Because she gets everything, and I get nothing," I said bitterly.

I didn't even care that I was making a lot of noise as I

stomped up the stairs, whose banister was wrapped in the garland I'd made by hand. I wasn't sneaking around my own goddamn house.

"The nerve of that man," I said angrily. "How dare he get her pregnant then give her my house—my life that we built together."

Even though I knew it was just going to ruin the rest of my holiday season, I swung open the door to the left of the stair landing.

"She even took my nursery." I sank down onto the floor. "That's the cradle my grandfather made right before he died. He was so excited for me to have a baby. She took all my furniture, and the will says she can have it."

"Emmie…" Marius sat on the floor of the nursery I'd spent years agonizing over, making sure it was perfect for the baby who was going to make it all worthwhile, a baby who was never going to come.

He gathered me into his strong arms.

Then I was breaking down and sobbing in Marius's arms. "I wanted a baby. That's all I wanted. I tried and tried."

Marius made comforting noises.

"Brooks said it was my fault, that I was defective as a woman, that I wasn't meant to be a mother."

"I see you with all those cats," Marius said in a low, soothing voice. "I think you'll be a wonderful mother."

"I don't know." I hiccupped, wiping at my eyes. "Brooks and I were trying forever, but I think I'm infertile." I sniffled. "We tried for a year and nothing. He hated me for not getting pregnant. He said he was fine… and it's true because Oakley is pregnant."

Marius's arms squeezed me tighter as I spoke into the soft wool of his suit.

"For a second, I thought about getting a sperm donor, but I don't have anywhere to live, and I bet it would just be a waste. I'm old, and I can't get pregnant. Clearly."

"You're not old, and you're not defective," Marius assured

me.

"You're my lawyer, not my friend. You don't have to pretend to be nice to me."

"I'm not being nice. You clearly don't know much about male anatomy." He tilted my chin up. "Brooks was cheating on you, right? Well, a man only produces so many elves a week, so to speak. If he was sending all the presents down someone else's chimney before he got to your house, then no babies for Christmas. I had a roommate who was looking at being a sperm donor but decided against it because you had to abstain from sex unless it was in a small, cold, windowless room, and he didn't want to waste his college years on that."

"So you think I could get pregnant?" My heart fluttered.

"I think you should try with someone who isn't cheating on you before you start catastrophizing." Marius petted my hair. "You're not paying me. That means I don't have to stoically watch a woman cry." He swung me to my feet. "Let's go to the Christmas market. I'll buy you some yarn. You can knit one of those cats a sweater."

"I need to find clues first."

Brooks's study was a disorganized mess. He'd never wanted me to clean it. Now I knew it was because he was hiding multiple affairs.

"Do you see any jewelry receipts?" I asked. "I bet that bracelet I found in my kitchen belongs to Oakley. We need to prove it."

"I don't see how you can find anything in this dump," Marius said, opening drawers.

In my craft room, which was almost as heart-wrenching as the nursery, Oakley had set up shop at my white desk with the brass trim.

Her laptop was open.

I opened up her search history and looked. She was searching for medicines that made someone sick.

I snapped a photo with my phone.

"Marius?" I wandered next door into the master bedroom, which was messy and smellier than I'd left it.

The lawyer was looking at something else. "Are these Brooks's clothes?" he asked me, pointing at a suit draped haphazardly over the chair in the master bedroom. "I didn't think he ever wore a suit."

"Kris Kringle on a shingle," I whispered. "Oakley is having an affair!" I jumped into his arms, hugging him and giving him a big kiss on the cheek. "And you say you're not a detective." I snapped my fingers. "Ooh, I bet that baby isn't Brooks's!"

CHAPTER 10
Marius

Emmie was happily sipping on the Christmas-themed drink I'd bought her.

"Yes, I need this!" She picked up a wooden hand-painted cat ornament.

"Buy two, get one free!" a lady chirped.

"Which other two do you want?" I asked Emmie.

She gaped up at me. "You can't just buy these for me."

"Sure I can."

"Well, which one do you—sorry. Never mind. Brooks would get mad when I asked him that question."

I let my hand rest on her back then trailed my fingers through her hair. "You forget I like cats."

"Brooks hated cats."

"It's well established that Brooks was an idiot in a number of ways," I told her. "Cats are amazing." I picked up one ornament. "This one looks like Moose."

"Aww, it's got his little snaggletooth. Do you think he's okay with the other cats?" Emmie turned to stare up at me.

"He's a Bengal cat, so I'll do anything to get some energy out of him. He's been playing hard with the other cats. He actually sleeps at night now," I joked.

"He needs a furry friend," Emmie said as the stall owner handed us the bag.

I ushered Emmie away.

I didn't need her looking too closely at the stall catty-corner to this one or draw the attention of its owner. We didn't need to muddy the waters.

"I don't think the feral-cat committee would appreciate that. They seem very anti adoption."

"Tell me about it." Emmie sighed. "I think a lot of them are animal hoarders masquerading as do-gooders. You should join the committee." She grabbed my hand. "We need—"

"Some fresh blood?"

She stuck her tongue out at me. "We need some sane people. Just me and Cora are the only ones."

"Rosie seems fine."

Emmie snatched her hand away.

I grabbed it again. "Someone's jealous."

"You're just my lawyer. You can go on a date with Rosie. I won't stop you."

I didn't let her tug away, just pulled her closer. It was nice to walk with a pretty girl in the snow. There was something wholesome about it.

"Rosie's not my type."

"You mean you don't like girls with big boobs and mouths that look like candy wrapped around your cock?" she asked bitterly.

"What the fuck?" I stopped abruptly, turning her around to face me.

"That's what Brooks always said."

"About Rosie?" I was taken aback. "He said that to you?"

"He was trying to convince me to get a boob job."

"You don't need..." I changed the subject and stared straight ahead so I didn't stare down at her chest. "The guy's dead, Emmie. You need to get him out of your head."

"It's too late," she forced out. "I think he's ruined me."

"I don't think so."

"Maybe I just need to solve the mystery and finally get closure." She pulled out the bracelet.

"This doesn't look like something from a typical jewelry store. I bet Brooks had a craftsman make it."

"So you're just going to ask every random jeweler?" I asked.

"Sure. Someone will know who did make it."

That kicked off a scavenger hunt through the Christmas market, from jeweler to custom jeweler. Finally, one located too close for comfort to the stall I was trying to avoid, looked at the bracelet with recognition.

"You made this?" I asked, incredulous, as I took in the messy piles of beads and gold wire in the stall.

"Oh no, not this one. This is a high-end piece!" the older woman exclaimed.

"Do you know who made it?" Emmie perked up.

"No, but"—she handed the bracelet back—"the girl will be so happy you found it." She chatted as she rifled through her stash. "She was such a nice girl, didn't have much money but had lost her favorite bracelet. I said I'd see what I could do. I didn't have much to go off of." The jeweler held up a bad copy of the bracelet Emmie had found. "She'll be so glad that you found the actual one."

"What was the girl's name?" I asked. "Was it Oakley?"

"Oh no. It was a plant name, though. I have it somewhere. Somewhere!" she sang, disappearing under the table, then came out with a scrap of paper.

"A-ha! Rosie was the girl."

CHAPTER 11
Emmie

"**N**o way." Zoe shook her head as we split the leftover lobster mac 'n' cheese she'd brought from Girl Meets Fig. "Rosie? I don't believe she'd kill Brooks. What's even the motive?"

"She loved him. He told her that he wasn't going to leave Oakley for her, and she offed him. Snuck into my kitchen, poisoned the cupcakes, brought them to him as a gift. He ate them because he's a pig, and then he came to my shop and croaked."

"If she did kill him, she did you a favor in more ways than one." Zoe speared another noodle.

It was true. The café had never been busier—even with the cat-committee protestors, there was a line down the block to go to the murder cat café. And we were doing a brisk business of cat adoption, though it never seemed to make a dent in the number of kitties in the shop. Maybe I had more cats than I thought.

There were so many customers that I'd hired on two of the young Svensson sisters, who were in town, visiting their brothers. They were working the cash register and making coffee like seasoned holiday-tourism pros.

"If you wouldn't potentially be on the hook for a murder, I'd say just leave it alone," Zoe added, scraping out the last of the cheese sauce with her spoon. "Let's go confront Rosie. I bet she caves."

"I don't think that's a good idea," I argued as I followed Zoe out of the shop and down Main Street. "What if she's not guilty and we start unnecessary rumors?"

"Jack-fucking-pot," Zoe murmured as we stopped in the doorway of the pungent-smelling Essence & Earth herbalist shop. "This place is nothing but poisons."

Little glass vials and bottles lined the light birchwood shelves on the walls. Soft spa music played from unseen speakers. The soothing atmosphere was disrupted by Rosie and Alice talking furiously in a corner.

I managed to catch Rosie saying, "He was poison to me," then an angry man yelled, causing them to jump away from each other.

Rosie smiled widely at me then glared at the man next to me. "Charles, you can't come in here and scare away the tourists."

"There's another cat in my shop!" he ranted.

"That one isn't one of my café cats," I countered. "You just stole a random person's cat."

"Yes, it is!" He shook the confused white cat at me.

Alice hurried by to scoop the kitty up in her arms.

"My cats have a custom-knitted collar," I informed him.

"Maybe the cat slipped it off," Charles blustered, "or maybe you removed it so you could gaslight me, try to make me think I'm crazy to take the heat off of you."

"You're the one with the motive, not Emmie," Zoe said hotly. "Murderer!"

Charles shot a final angry look at us, muttered, then scuttled off back to his shop, almost bowling over a confused Marius.

"What happened?"

"Petty small-town drama." I sighed.

Marius had a protective hand on my lower back.

"We didn't get to interrogate Rosie," Zoe argued as Marius tugged me back outside onto Main Street.

"Save it for later. I just got the toxicology reports back," he said in a low voice.

My eyes widened.

"It's not good. They found trace amounts of cyanide."

"Brooks was murdered. Oh my God!"

"Cyanide is used to clean jewelry," Zoe said flatly, "and Rosie was just at a jewelry shop. Means, motive, and opportunity. Boom. It also has an almond smell, which would be disguised in a baked good."

"Charles is a more likely suspect at this point." Marius shook his head. "He hates you, snuck into your kitchen, put cyanide in the cupcakes, then tried to frame you for Brooks's murder to get your café shut down."

"Someone put cyanide in my cupcakes. Oh my God. *Oh my God.* I don't know why I'm acting like this," I said, suddenly feeling lightheaded. I'd been hoping it was all a big mistake and that Brooks had just had a heart attack or something.

I tried to rally. I wasn't Marius's girlfriend; he didn't need to deal with my emotional state on top of my legal case.

"The police don't have this information yet," Marius added in a low voice. "Though I suspect at some point they're going to do their own tests."

"So we need to prove my innocence like *now* now." Then I had a thought. "What else did the report find?"

"Nothing? Cyanide?" He gave me a questioning look.

"Like, what were the ingredients used in the cream filling and the cupcake and the frosting?"

"Yeah, maybe someone passed off a store-bought cupcake as yours." Zoe grabbed me.

"I'll have more tests run," Marius promised. "Until then, you need to be careful. We're not sure who the real target is, and there's a murderer out there."

CHAPTER 12
Marius

"I'm not giving you any lip, Aunt Frances." I fought an ugly battle with myself to keep my face pleasantly neutral.

"Good, because I'm not asking for much. Costco is right down the road. Won't take you long at all to stop in and get a few little things I need."

"No one needs a candle in a ten-gallon bucket, Aunt Frances."

"Myra's granddaughter bought her one. Make sure you get the red-and-white-striped one. I'll take the green one, but don't bring one of the blue ones back."

"You're driving out in this?" Emmie asked me when I walked through the great room, keys in hand.

Moose didn't even look up from where he was napping in front of the fire. Snow fell softly outside, coating everything in white.

Emmie tucked a lock of her hair behind her ear.

"Apparently, my great-aunt desperately needs a candle."

"She'll be the queen of the retirement community with one of those." Emmie chuckled.

"I have to get going. I'm sure Costco closes soon."

"It's the holidays. They unofficially stay open late."

"Joy."

"I can come with you… if you want the company." Emmie was giving me that soft smile again.

"Come on." I jerked my head.

"I can't believe you have a car in New York City," she said as I helped her with her coat.

"The only reason is that my company provides free parking, so I just keep my car in the company deck," I admitted as I opened the door of the black sedan for her.

I turned on the heat in the frigid car, brushed the snow off the windshield, then we were off, driving in the snowy dark down Gingerbread Lane.

"I thought it was Wisteria Lane." I frowned.

"The street changes seasonally for the holidays or whenever one of the seniors has a whim. Mrs. Abercrombe still does part-time work at city hall in the mayor's office. She changes the name for them. The seniors always throw a party for the name change. Yes, it's extremely confusing for everyone. But it does give the postman job security."

"You've been here awhile," I said to her, glancing briefly in the dark.

"Six months." Emmie sighed heavily. "And no end in sight. Nor any suspects."

"We have lots of suspects, just no evidence."

The Costco parking lot outside of town was busier than I'd expected.

Inside, a fight was about to break out over the last package of Christmas lights. I just kept walking toward the candle display. I didn't want to be involved.

I shook my head as Emmie's eyes sparkled at the comically oversize candles.

"Who needs a candle this size? Aunt Frances is going to be dead before she can even burn half of it."

"Don't say that!" Emmie cried, trying to roll the massive candle onto the cart.

It lurched, almost hitting a man.

"I'm sorry!" Emmie exclaimed.

The man, with his eyes hidden by sunglasses, a hoodie pulled up around his face, and a baseball cap low on his forehead, swore then took off at a run down the nearest aisle.

I caught a whiff of almonds.

"That's him—the guy who was breaking into your shop. It's the murderer."

"Wait!" Emmie called as I sprinted after the murderer.

I ran after him down the dog-food aisle, sliding at the end. I caught a movement to my left and took off down an aisle with bakeware. "Dammit!" I swore as, out of nowhere, a box of Christmas ornaments was hurled at me.

I knocked it out of the way.

The murderer squawked and jumped out from behind a stack of flat-screen TVs.

But he was too slow.

I tackled him, sending us crashing into a display of Frosty the Snowman puppets.

"Don't touch me! Don't hurt me!" The smaller man tried to wiggle away.

"You…" Emmie puffed, pushing the squeaky cart in front of her. "Have really long legs. Oh, you caught the murderer! And you thought you were going to get away with it, didn't you… Charles?" Emmie yelped as she pulled the hat off.

"Knew it," I said. "I told you he was up to no good. Call the cops."

"No, please!" Charles cried. "I beg of you. Yes, I admit what I did was wrong, but I can explain."

"Murder is never okay."

"Murder?" Charles made a strangled noise. "I didn't murder anyone."

"Then why were you running?" Emmie demanded. "Why were you sneaking into my café?"

"I wasn't stealing from you—I swear it. I wasn't even in your café. I needed my shop to capitalize on the Santa Claws Café being shut down. I sell cream buns. But"—he gestured helplessly—"I don't know how to bake. I buy premade pastry from Costco, fill them with a pudding and Cool Whip mixture, then sell it at a markup. I can't make a stable cream filling to save my life, and you can forget about buttercream frosting." Charles started to sob.

I let him get up.

"Please don't call the cops. I'm not a thief or a murderer."

"Just a fraud," Emmie said determinedly.

CHAPTER 13
Emmie

"Well, that's a suspect crossed off our list."

"Too bad he was my number-one pick," Marius said as he unloaded three of the massive candles in the back of his trunk along with a pack of light bulbs to replace the broken one in the alley behind my café.

I hadn't even asked him—he'd just picked them up.

Brooks would never have done that.

To be fair, any man looked great compared to Brooks.

Especially since Brooks is dead, I thought hysterically.

"I don't believe him about breaking into your shop, though. Both you and I saw him in your alley."

"We saw someone," I said uncertainly. "Maybe Charles is telling the truth."

"If he is," Marius said as he started the car, "who was breaking into your shop, and who murdered Brooks?"

"You don't have to keep spending time with me, you know," I told Marius. "You already rescued me from a jail cell and bought me a candle."

My new giant candle had been overtaken by cats, several of which were napping in it.

Marius's Bengal cat was hissing at a big white one.

"I thought you were giving some of these away for adoption." Marius frowned and handed me a plastic bag.

"You don't have to keep giving me gifts. I know I'm not your girlfriend, just your charity case. You probably have lots of women falling all over you in the city."

He gave me a slightly pained smile. "Not exactly. They all want hedge fund managers or big-time lawyers. I'm a corporate lawyer with in-house legal. That's seen as, like, the mommy track because I work normal hours. I like to have a life. I don't want to be a slave to my job. I like having time to be able to help people. Not cupcake murderers"— he nudged me—"but like an underemployed single mom who can't afford a lawyer for her kid who was just in the wrong place at the wrong time. I want time to spend with my family and friends. That's seen as being not committed among the type-A lawyers in the city who pull one-hundred-hour weeks."

"Yikes." I grimaced. "I'm sure that works for some people, but I like to be home at a reasonable hour."

"Exactly. I've worked for a ton of big shot lawyers. With them, it's all work all the time, then they wake up in their forties and fifties, and their kids don't talk to them, they're on wife number three, and their pets act like they're strangers."

"Well, thank you anyway." I held up the bag. "It means a lot to me—not just the gifts but all of it. Your time—"

"This isn't a gift—it's Brooks's personal effects. As his wife, you're entitled to them. The police released them to you. They kept his phone," Marius told me. "For evidence."

I slowly emptied the bag onto the counter. His watch. A pack of gum. A small blue box...

"He was going to propose to Oakley." I bit back the tears. "Because she's the mother of his child."

Marius took the box out of my hands, set it on the counter, and cupped my face. "Trust me. You dodged a bullet. You're better off not being that monster's brood mare. There are a number of sane men out there who would love to call you their wife and give you the family and children you always dreamed of."

Is it crazy that, for a moment, I was hoping he'd say, "And one of those men is me"?

"Are you sure you still want to attend the town hall meeting?" Marius asked, buttoning up his long wool overcoat.

"I always go to the town halls," I said firmly, "and I won't have the murderer driving me off."

I wondered if maybe I should have skipped this one when I walked into the crowded historic city hall building. The interior had been decorated for Christmas. Along one side, Zoe had set up the catering and was yelling at the townspeople to back off, only one cup of punch per person.

"Be careful," I warned Marius when he was handed a glass. "It's spiked."

"You're such a good friend," Gran was saying to Beatrice, "to fetch Oakley a snack. Her baby's due soon, and I remember how hard it was to get around at her size."

If I wasn't mistaken, anger flashed on Beatrice's face when Gran said that.

"Yes, well, we do have to help our friends when they're in need, and if you're in need, they return the favor."

"Sometimes," Cora added then reddened.

Beatrice shot her a nasty look. "Yes, sometimes." She stalked off.

Gran grabbed Marius's arm and started talking his ear off.

I wanted to press Cora for info about Beatrice. "How's she doing?" I asked. "You guys are friends, right? Beatrice doesn't seem her usual self."

"I think Oakley's running her ragged," Cora admitted to me under her breath as I accepted two spinach pastries and a cup of punch.

Over on the other side of the hall, Oakley, with hands clasped firmly on her belly, was berating Beatrice about the food she'd brought her.

"Beatrice is probably sad about Brooks too," I said lightly.

"Oh?"

"Well, they were all *close* friends," I said, hoping she'd take the hint and spill a clue. "You know, always hanging out, going off to remote cabins together. Women were always attracted to Brooks. Football captain, homecoming king."

We wound our way to our seats.

"I'd say you could sit next to us," Cora said to me, "but I don't think Alice and Gertrude are going to like that."

"Yoo-hoo!" Gran waved from where Marius was sitting stoically in his seat. She patted the chair next to her.

There was shuffling of the seniors, then I was sitting right next to Marius. The chairs in the town hall were narrow, and Marius was not a small man. Even though I scrunched up in my seat, my leg kept inadvertently bumping his, then I'd panic.

The third time I almost spilled the punch on his bespoke suit, he grabbed my knee, his hand warm through my tights.

I chugged the rest of my punch, feeling a little woozy from the rum and whatever else was in there.

"Order!" Mayor Meghan Loring called out, banging her gavel on the lectern. "Order!"

The loud talking quieted.

"Merry Christmas, everyone. We'd like to remind everyone that the tourists are guests in our quaint historic town of Harrogate, and we need to make them feel welcome. That does not mean fleecing them for murder tours," she said to several unrepentant blond teenage boys.

Her husband, Hunter Svensson, stood over them, his face stony.

"Before we move on to new business… yes, Ida, the sex festival in tandem with the Valentine's Day market is on the agenda, but just be warned it does not have the support of the council."

"Send it to a referendum!" Ida demanded.

"That is new business," Meghan said firmly. "The first old-business item: the feral-cat colonies."

The feral-cat committee members jumped up and started chanting in the middle of the hall. "Cats belong in compost, not café!"

Marius stood up. "Excuse me. Is this town seriously advocating killing cats and throwing them into compost piles?" Marius's courtroom voice—smooth, assured—carried throughout the hall.

Several townspeople started muttering and glaring at the feral-cat committee.

Townspeople who'd gotten there early and were on their third round of punch started throwing napkins and empty paper cups at Gertrude and Alice.

"It seems to me," Marius continued, "that the Santa Claws Café has found a wonderful way to help these cats find homes. I understand it's a pilot program, however. It needs to be expanded. There have been multiple complaints from businesses on Main Street about the unhoused cats. Charles, I believe you had issues with rogue feral cats?"

Charles gulped and squeaked out, "Yes," then half covered his face.

"Perhaps the mayor would like to put her name on an initiative for more cat cafés to help all needy cats find homes this Christmas," Marius said to Meghan.

"That boy is smooth," Gran whispered. "Bet he does anal like that too."

I was not thinking about that this Christmas.

"The feral-cat committee is firmly against cat cafés!" Gertrude said shrilly.

"Shut up, you cat hoarder," Ida booed. "You all constantly ask for donations, and there are cats everywhere, running amok in town. It's not even a cool animal like the town of Waverly, which has all those chickens. Cats don't lay eggs."

"More cat cafés!" Zoe chanted form the back of the room. "Cats belong in cafés, not compost piles!"

The rest of the crowd drunkenly joined in.

Marius was smug when he sat back down.

The mayor called for a second to vote on expanding the area for cat cafés, provided they be geared for adoption.

I noticed the angry looks Gertrude and Alice were giving me.

Murderous looks, one might say.

CHAPTER 14
Marius

’d only had half a glass of that punch, and I had a splitting headache when I woke up the next morning, partially smothered by Moose, who had draped himself over my chin.

"Off." I pushed the cat away and stumbled through my great-aunt's small apartment.

"When you have a baby, I hope you're not going to let that cat smother the poor mite," Aunt Frances told me disapprovingly as I blearily searched for coffee.

"What baby?" I sat down hard in the kitchen chair, and she handed me a cup of coffee.

"You're not even trying. You're a catch! Women in this town are throwing themselves at you. You could be engaged by Christmas if you wanted," Aunt Frances railed. "I don't know how much longer I have left in this world."

"That's what got me in trouble the last time," I reminded her dryly. "I am not falling for that again."

"Well, shit. If you're out today, go buy me a lottery ticket at least."

"What kind of lawyer are you, buying a lottery ticket?" Emmie tapped me on the arm when I was in line at Ida's general store.

"Buying boxed cake mix?" I teased her.

She hit me lightly. "Shh! You'll start the gossip mill, and then where will my twenty cats and I go?" She held up a bright-yellow package. "I need to hack Brooks's watch."

"What?"

"Brooks's watch was one of those fancy smartwatches. I don't know the password, but I found this YouTube video that tells you how to crack into a smartwatch. Then I can read his text messages," Emmie said excitedly.

I grabbed the little child's-magnet-science kit. "That is not going to work. I'll send it out to some of my techs in New York."

"I feel like I already owe you a lot." She wrinkled her nose.

It was cute.

"You don't owe me anything."

"Yes, I do," she insisted. "After this is over, I'm going to really spoil you. I'll make all your favorite foods, do your laundry, clean your bathroom, give you massages on demand..."

I raised an eyebrow, making her stammer.

"A massage, like a spa-day massage, not..."

"Too bad." I winked at her.

She gaped as I paid for the lottery tickets. "Do you, in your lawyerly opinion, think that we're getting closer?"

"Closer to solving the murder? Not really," I told Emmie. "Closer to having evidence where a jury would find you not guilty? Depends."

"On what?" she asked desperately.

"On if the trial stays in Harrogate or if the county takes it over."

"Oh."

"Where are the magnets?" Zoe asked when we walked into the café.

"Marius is sending it out to his special secret crime laboratory." Emmie gave me that smile like I was her entire world.

"It's not that secret. They have a website."

"And how long will that take?" Zoe demanded.

"A week, maybe? If they're not backed up. I'll have to check," I said with a shrug.

"Not soon enough."

"This isn't the movies," I told Zoe. "These things take time."

Zoe thrust the watch at Emmie. "You lived with this motherfucker for years. What's his pin code?"

Emmie made a helpless gesture.

"You're going to lock it," I warned.

"Brooks is… well, *was* dumb," Zoe said. "He probably used the same pin for everything."

"He didn't like me going near his laptop." Emmie chewed her lip.

"Probably because he was sending nudes to half of the women in Harrogate." Zoe sniffed. "It needs a six-figure pin code. Birthday? Anniversary?"

"I highly doubt it."

"You only get three attempts before you're locked out," I warned again.

"It could be anything," Emmie fretted.

Zoe rubbed her hands together then picked up the watch and typed in a code.

"What are you—" I reached for the watch. The guys couldn't hack it if it was locked.

"In!" Zoe crowed. "Thirty-six, twenty-four, thirty-six, baby, because your ex was a basic-ass Brandon." She scrolled through the miniscule text messages on the smartwatch. "Here are the messages to Oakley."

"Anything incriminating, like, 'I know you're about to murder me'?" Emmie asked dejectedly.

"No, just a lot of whining and complaining about how much money she's spending on shopping. Oh, look at that. *Quelle surprise.* He was cheating on Oakley."

"Those are explicit," Emmie said, picking at her fingernails as Zoe scrolled through the text messages between Brooks and someone he had labeled Tits in his contacts. The messages were borderline pornographic.

I gave Emmie a concerned look. Her face was blanched, lips pressed tight as she and Zoe skimmed the messages for a clue about who this person was.

"Whose number is it?" I asked.

Emmie checked it in her phone. "No one I know. It is a Harrogate area code, though."

"Are you all right?" I asked Emmie, tentatively cupping a hand on the back of her head.

"I'm fine." She nodded.

Zoe was scrolling through the rest of Brooks's contacts.

"I bet he told Theo who it was," I said. "He could never resist bragging."

"This thread is with Theo. Just a lot of misspellings. The literacy levels in this country really have gone to hell."

"Brooks could never read well," I interjected.

"You knew him?" Emmie was surprised.

I cursed inwardly. "Just in school. You know, small town. Everyone knows of everyone."

"Jack-fucking-pot!" Zoe whooped, saving me from more prying questions from Emmie. "Look at that. That is a motive for murder!"

> **Theo:** *You've been saying for months you're going to get me my money back.*
> **Brooks:** *You know I'm good for it.*
> **Theo:** *Just pay me back.*

"Why would Theo kill Brooks if he owed him money? He'd want him to pay it back."

"Maybe he couldn't."

I frowned. "Then you'd think they would get in an argument because Brooks can't pay and start fighting, and maybe Theo accidentally punches him too hard. This was premeditated. Brooks was poisoned."

"Theo can make a claim against the estate for unpaid debts if Brooks is dead," Zoe argued.

"Yeah, but how much money are we talking?" I argued. "No one's going to plan a murder over a thousand dollars. But a hundred thousand? That's a different story."

"Does it say how much money?" Emmie asked.

"Nope."

"I think," Emmie said slowly, "we need to go back to my house and look for more clues."

CHAPTER 15

Emmie

peeped in through the windows. The house was dark. I slowly slid my key into the lock and opened the door as silently as I could. Oakley's car wasn't outside, but you could never be too careful.

"If there are any clues, they'll be upstairs in the study," I whispered.

"Good luck finding anything in there," Marius muttered.

"Think positive," I hissed.

This was closer than I'd been to finding the real killer since Brooks had died. He and Theo having a beef over money? That was a way better motive than my being pissed about him in a new relationship six months after he'd kicked me out of my own house.

We crept up the stairs. Suddenly, there was a loud wail.

Marius grabbed me, clapping a hand over my mouth and smothering me against his chest before I could scream.

Zoe was unfazed. "Was that a cat?"

There was the noise again, this time accompanied by moaning and the telltale slap-slapping of someone getting it on.

"Oakley, take it, take my fucking cum, *yeah*," a male voice groaned as he apparently dumped all the presents down the chimney.

"Oh, Theo, give me your seed. I can't wait to have your baby. Oh, your cum feels so good in my pussy."

"Jesus Christ," Zoe muttered.

"They were in on it! Both of them murdered Brooks, and I am going to get my proof," I hissed.

Marius grabbed me as soon as I started to go up the stairs. "No. You're going to get caught."

"I need a photo. This is evidence. This will clear my name."

In the bedroom, the floor creaked as people began moving around.

"We're leaving. *Now*." Marius picked me up and carried me out of the house, shutting the front door behind all of us.

* * *

"You should have let me get a photo," I complained when we were celebrating with holiday-themed cocktails in the Christmas market. "Oakley is having an affair with Theo. This is means, motive, and opportunity all in one."

"It's a bad look if we all get arrested," Marius argued.

"Can't we just"—Zoe reached for a beef Wellington bite—"you know, anonymously send the news of the affair to the police?"

"This isn't TV. That's not how this works. That's not how any of this works." Marius stared vacantly at his cocktail.

"Someone's glad he volunteered for the Emmie-innocence shit show." Zoe laughed.

"Maybe my anonymous tip will convince the cops to search the house and find actual evidence," I argued. "They never searched the house, just Gran's apartment. She's still mad they messed up her fiddle-leaf fig. Also, I forgot. She wanted me to ask you if you could sue the police station on her behalf."

"Isn't that thing dead?" Zoe frowned. "And she painted it green in her art class?"

"So no, I won't be suing," Marius said slowly.

I slurped my drink thoughtfully. "Okay, new theory. The baby is not Brooks's, and Oakley offed him with the help of her affair partner."

"Theo is the murderer," Zoe said matter-of-factly. "Girl sleeps with boyfriend's best friend. Brooks finds out, and they off him for the money. It's practically a cliché. That would explain the motive."

"We needed a photo of them together for proof."

Marius shot me a glare. "If the paternity test comes back negative," he said, steepling his hands, "then that's all the proof we need."

"Or one of Brooks's *other* affair partners found out about the affair and was trying to kill Oakley with cupcakes," Zoe suggested.

"Pregnant women like cupcakes." Marius shrugged. "Maybe Oakley had a craving, and the other affair partner knew about it and exploited that knowledge."

"Beatrice. She's close enough to Oakley to know her cravings."

I ignored the twinge of sympathy I felt for Oakley. "Maybe Oakley was the intended victim after all."

CHAPTER 16
Marius

I took the long way through the Christmas market to my car, trying to clear my head.

It worked...

No, it didn't, I argued with myself. *It's complete bullshit.*

The stall seemed to materialize in front of me, a void that swallowed up the rest of the lights in the Christmas market.

This wasn't where the stall was yesterday, my mind unhelpfully told me. I walked toward it as if I was being reeled in.

It was just because I was distracted by Emmie—the sweet, homey Christmas smell of her, the soft curves, the way she fit perfectly in my arms.

"A happy voodoo-doll customer," the black-haired woman said.

I whirled around. I could have sworn she hadn't been there a minute ago.

Chimes sounded faintly, and smoke from incense hung hazily around us. In Lilith's arms was a black cat with yellow eyes.

"Have you come for another?" she asked.

"I don't believe in voodoo."

"And yet you spent quite a lot of money for that doll."

"I didn't kill Brooks."

"Then where is the doll?" Black eyes bored into mine. "I'll give you a refund."

"I don't have it."

I didn't have it because I had hidden it in the grocery sack of stuff Aunt Frances had asked me to get from Costco... including the toxic-mildew cleaner she'd wanted me to buy that had spilled in the bag, ruining the doll.

I'd discovered it late that night after getting Emmie out of jail.

"Then why don't I make you a new one," Lilith offered with a sharp smile. "On the house. Maybe for Brooks's friend—Theo, was it? Or maybe Oakley, who broke your heart?"

"No, I'm not a murderer." I stepped back.

"Everyone is a murderer when they're pushed far enough."

The black cat hissed at me, baring sharp fangs as I stumbled out of the stall.

I stood in the middle of the bright, cheery Christmas market as the pounding in my ears subsided. A witchy cackling under the tinny sound of Christmas carols made me involuntarily shiver.

I am eating too much rich holiday food, I decided, blotting at my sweating forehead.

I didn't kill Brooks. I know I didn't, right?

Then why was it temping to go back and slap down hundreds of dollars for two more dolls?

I needed grounding. My nerves were too fried to go back to the senior center, even though I was behind on work.

I needed Emmie—Emmie with her pretty face with its soft, kissable mouth, her cozy sweaters, and her warm hands so small in mine.

Emmie was closing up the café when I pulled my car up in front of her store.

"Marius!" she exclaimed when I gathered her in my arms. "What's wrong?" She squeezed me tight like it was the most natural thing in the world.

I buried my face in her hair, never wanting to let her go. "Nothing," I mumbled. "I just missed you."

"You only just met me," she said with a breathy laugh.

I leaned back, gazing down at her. I wanted to kiss her.

Or maybe whatever it was Lilith had put in that smoke was making me crazy.

A hungry meow sounded from Emmie's feet.

"I was going to take Moose back to your aunt's," she explained.

I tucked a piece of her hair behind her ear.

"I think he'd rather stay with you than in the cat hostel." She wrinkled her nose.

I leaned down to nuzzle her briefly, wishing I could press my mouth to hers.

My heart was still racing. I settled for wrapping an arm tightly around her waist.

"Let me take you out to dinner," I offered.

"You don't have to. You've gone above and beyond."

"I want to." I looked down at her, deciding, fuck it, actually I would kiss her. This had been the week of terrible life choices and, aggravatingly, reverting to the person I'd been in high school, so why the hell not?

"Let me take you out," I murmured, cupping her cheek, leaning in…

Angry yowls sounded as Moose took off, harness jingling as he raced into the dark alley.

"Moose, no!" I yelled, swearing as I ran after him, Emmie behind me.

"It's probably just a rat he heard," Emmie called after me as I advanced cautiously in the dark alley.

"I thought I replaced that light," I hissed as Emmie's phone flashlight shone into the alley.

Instead of a rat, though, Moose was yowling and spitting as he cornered a dark figure.

Emmie screamed when she realized what Moose was doing.

The figure was trying to escape, but he couldn't because of Moose and his sharp teeth and claws.

"And they say you need a dog if you want protection." I grabbed the smaller figure and hauled them up to slam them against the metal door to Emmie's kitchen. There was that smell of almonds. "Returning to the scene of the crime." I pulled at the hood and cap hiding their face.

Emmie exclaimed in surprise as the murderer dropped the spray bottle they were carrying and started sobbing. "I'm so sorry. I just didn't know what to do. I was pushed to the edge. I was in over my head. I was overwhelmed!"

"Alice?" Emmie peered at her fellow feral-cat-committee member.

"Please don't tell Gertrude," the other woman sobbed.

"I don't understand. Why did you kill Brooks?" I frowned.

"I didn't kill him." Alice was taken aback. "I didn't have anything to do with the murder."

"Then what are you doing here, smelling like cyanide?"

"Oh, this?" Alice picked up the spray bottle. "It was just to help the café cats accept the new cats."

"New cats?"

Moose was hissing and spitting at the large plastic box near the door. Out of one of the holes in the plastic box, a paw reached.

"The white cat. You've been dumping cats here," Emmie said accusingly. "After you protested in front of my shop and called me a murderer, *you're* the one abandoning cats."

"I'm not abandoning them. They're going to a good home!" Alice wailed. "Gertrude..." She lowered her voice. "She keeps stopping by with more cats for me to keep in my house. It's too much. It's too many cats, and you're adopting them out, Emmie. I didn't think you'd notice."

"Moose noticed," I said.

"Charles did too." Emmie pressed her lips together.

"Some of them didn't quite make it into your shop," Alice admitted. "Oh, please, *please* don't tell Gertrude. I'll call off the protests. Just... I cannot take these cats back. My house is overrun. And you're doing such a great job adopting them out. I think Cora's going to open a cat diner or something, and she can take some. Oh, Gertrude is so mad about the town hall." Alice wrung her hands.

"This is absolute madness," I muttered.

"Do you think you could take these cats?" Alice asked hopefully.

Emmie sighed, and I picked up the carrier, much to Moose's annoyance.

"Did you," I asked as Alice started to dart away out of the alley, "happen to see anything suspicious while you were out here sneaking around at night?"

Alice blinked. "I've seen Rosie out late."

"Doesn't her shop stay open late?" Emmie said.

"Only during the holidays. Earlier this year? Not so much, but she'd be out. I thought it was suspicious because she wasn't dressed for cat catching."

CHAPTER 17

Emmie

"We need to just confront her," I said, barging into Marius's great-aunt's apartment. Frances was out at bingo night with my grandmother. I knew I shouldn't bother Marius, but I could feel it. We were close to solving this thing.

"Confront who?" he asked.

I walked into the kitchen, where he was standing shirtless at the sink with a big tub of soapy water, giving Moose a bath. "You bathe your cat?"

"Yeah, because you clearly don't," he said. "They all reek of that almond spray."

"You ever tried to bathe a cat?" I complained.

Then it hit me.

Marius was standing in front of me with no, *zero*, shirt on.

Droplets of water from where the cat had splashed him clung to his chiseled chest. The muscles in his forearm worked as he shampooed the black-and-gold cat's head.

"Guess he doesn't sit in front of a computer all day," I croaked.

Marius gave me an odd look.

I tried not to think about how he'd almost kissed me.

"You still owe me dinner," the deep voice purred.

"Of course! I'll cook for you anytime."

"No," he said, fishing the sopping-wet cat out of the bucket. "I still want to take you to dinner."

Forget dinner—I wanted him to take me to bed.

He was literally all my favorite things in one perfect Christmas package as he stood there in front of me, just in the dress pants and barefoot, cradling his cat to his chest in a towel as he gently dried him off.

Marius kissed Moose's little velvet nose.

My heart clenched.

My ovaries exploded.

"You'll, um…" I stammered, "have to teach me your tricks."

"You want to hop into a bath with me…?"

"Yes."

"And bathe a cat?"

Minus the cat? Yes, right now.

He looked down at Moose. The Bengal cat extended his neck to give Marius a kitty kiss.

Ugh, so freaking adorable.

The man's and the cat's eyes were almost the same green-gold color.

I am not thinking about all that shifter-romance soft-core porn I consumed after my breakup.

"I, um… think we should do it tomorrow."

"The bath?" he asked.

My ovaries started building him a shrine.

"Uh, the confronting of Rosie?"

The toweling of Moose paused.

"If she *is* the murderer, I don't think that's a good idea."

⁂

"So, I think my fertility issues are cured. I felt my ovaries wake up from the infinite boot loop they were stuck in," I said to Zoe, sitting down across from her at Girl Meets Fig. It was early for the restaurant, but the Santa Claws Café was hopping. The Svensson sisters were excellent at being shop girls and also seemed to be unnervingly good at coercing tips from people.

"You never had fertility issues," Zoe countered as we shared the leftover twice-baked potato bites from dinner service the previous day. "You had a shitty piece of shit of a husband, and your ovaries were looking out for you. Now that you have a hottie who likes cats and has a job, the baby-making factory is back in business."

"Marius doesn't just have a job—he has a smoking-hot body." I sighed then looked down at my own stomach and thighs. Even when I was at my thinnest, Gran liked to assure me I was sturdy.

"Gran always said you need a working-class guy. She'd advise, like, a roofer or an electrician. They like a girl with some meat on her bones. 'Honest men like honest women,'" I said, quoting Gran. "Marius isn't a firefighter or even blue-collar adjacent. He's used to those New York City women."

"What guy doesn't like tits and ass?" Zoe countered. "Brooks is dead, gone, and buried. Don't let his ghost live rent-free in your head, fucking up your self-esteem. Marius was absolutely flirting with you. He literally asked you out."

"I don't know…"

"He was bathing a cat shirtless. He was *so* doing that on purpose."

"He said he doesn't sleep with clients anyway."

"He's a lawyer. He's probably already found the loophole to exploit. I bet he just wants to make sure you're not going to freak out and report him to the bar." Zoe glared at me. "You aren't, right?"

"I'm not reporting him."

"No freaking out either?"

"Maybe." I chewed on my lip. "Maybe I need to just concentrate on clearing my name. I've only been a widow a week."

"Funny," Zoe said flatly, "because Brooks has been dead to me for the past three years."

"Maybe Marius was right," I hissed as we stood outside of the Essence & Earth herbalist.

"No, we put her on the spot. I can tell when people are lying. You don't know how many times people used to stiff us at Girl Meets Fig. My grandmother would believe any sob story. Not me. Let's go."

My friend wrenched the door open and marched in.

Rosie looked up from where she was packing sparkling little vials into gift baskets for Christmas presents that people could buy premade.

Zoe marched right up to the counter and slapped the bracelet onto the countertop. "Recognize this?"

"My bracelet!" Rosie cried. "I mean, uh…" Her eyes darted between Zoe and me. "I've never seen that before in my life. What a lovely piece of jewelry."

"Save it. We know it belongs to you," Zoe snapped. "Why did you kill Brooks?"

"I didn't! I'd never hurt Pookie!"

Barf.

Zoe made a gagging noise.

"I love Brooks."

"And he said he would never leave Oakley for you, and you killed him."

"I'd never! I was heartbroken when he died. He was the only man I ever loved," she sobbed.

"He was literally cheating on you with other women he was cheating on his wife with. It's like a Christmas wreath of cheating," Zoe said, drawing a circle in the air.

"I know, and I'm sorry," Rosie said to me. "I didn't get with him until after you and he split. He said he was tired of Oakley, that she was being too demanding and emotional. He said she stopped getting all dressed up for him, and they barely had sex anymore. He was desperate. He didn't love her. He was just with her because of the baby." Rosie reached for the bracelet.

I snatched it back. "He used my money to pay for it."

Rosie gave me a hurt look. "I'd never harm him; we were in love."

"Are you sure?" I asked, thinking back to Beatrice taking a lock of his hair. "I guess Beatrice was snipping a lock of hair off Brooks's corpse to give to you as a memento, then."

Rosie's eyes went wide, then her lips curled back. "That man-stealing bitch."

"You dodged a bullet," I told her kindly.

Her face went cold. "I think you need to leave now."

"If she wasn't a murderer then, she is now," I joked as we headed into the Christmas market.

I needed nourishment, and the cupcake shop was a zoo.

The Christmas market wasn't all that much better. We hurried to get in line at the Merry Munchies for a ho-ho hog roast sandwich, limited time only. Darren had gone out and hunted it himself last weekend.

"The person Brooks was texting has to be Beatrice, what with the stealing of a lock of hair from his literal corpse," Zoe decided.

"That is clearly the action of someone who can commit murder." I nodded as we hurried through the crowded market.

"Guess what!" Zoe said, looking at her phone. "Beatrice just started a new job at Svensson PharmaTech. She'd have access to cyanide."

I looked over her shoulder, reading the LinkedIn app page.

I grunted when we ran into someone.

"I'm so sorry!" Cora exclaimed as I stumbled.

"I was meaning to talk to you. But not like this!" I joked.

"Oh yeah?"

"With the new cat café law expansion, Alice said you might want to open a sister cat café for adoption. I have some info here," I told her, fumbling in my purse.

Brooks's watch tumbled out along with my wallet.

Cora reached down for it.

"I'd love to!" she said then looked down at the watch in her hand. "Early Christmas present? From a certain lawyer perhaps?"

"It's Brooks's; we're looking for murder clues. Seems like Oakley wasn't the only person he was cheating on me with." I took the watch back.

"How a man as dumb as Brooks could juggle three affair partners is astounding," Zoe said dryly. "The women of Harrogate truly have no self-respect."

"How horrible for you, Emmie," Cora said, her eyes wide.

"Well, keep me posted on the cat café."

"The ho-ho hog roast was worth the wait," I said as we made our way back to the café, eating and window shopping.

The air dropped by ten degrees as a black cat crossed my path.

I shivered. "Are you lost, little guy?"

The cat hissed and did that weird thing cats do where they crab walk sideways like they're possessed by the devil.

"Salem, did you find us a customer?"

Smokey incense wafted out of a stall.

"'Sup, Lilith?" Zoe asked the town's resident potential witch and purveyor of the only decent spices you could get in Harrogate.

"I hope you didn't come to finally take me up on the offer of the voodoo doll," the black-haired woman said.

"Maybe we could go ahead and buy it," Zoe mused. "You know, it could help you process your cheating husband's untimely death, especially if he fucks you out of your own house."

"As much as I would have like to sell you the doll, it's gone. I can make another." One of her black fingernails trailed along the shelves filled with creepy Victorian artifacts.

"We'd have to do a little grave robbing." Lilith smiled like that was all she'd ever wanted in the world. "Or we could make one of a living person. Perhaps Oakley. Or one of the other women who were sleeping with your husband."

"I don't have disposable income to spend on voodoo dolls that don't work. I need to up my spice order. The cardamom buns are flying off the shelves," I said firmly.

"Oh, they work." Lilith's eyes were pools of black.

"I didn't kill him, if that's what you're implying," I said sharply.

"I know you didn't kill him." She stroked the black cat with a pale hand. "I know who did, though." She flashed an enigmatic smile.

"Who?" I choked out. "I need proof." Suddenly, the thought that this could all be over was overwhelming.

"The man who bought Brooks's voodoo doll made with hair and nails you gave me."

"Who?" Zoe demanded.

"Marius."

"That's absurd." I barked out a laugh. "Just tell me how much for the extra spices."

"Ask your grandmother why a man who dresses like a boring corporate drone is buying a voodoo doll." She pulled out a deck of tarot cards. "Read your fortune?"

"No, thank you. You can scam tourists but not me."

I had another sandwich in my bag for Marius. It was getting cold as we walked quickly through the market.

"Voodoo dolls."

"We should ask her for one of him but, like, a sex-doll version." Zoe cackled.

"I don't need a sex doll."

"Why? Did you sleep with him?"

"No! He's my lawyer. We're not like that."

Except for the dinner invitation and the cuddling on Main Street...

"What?" I asked Zoe.

"Ida saw you and told my grandmother," Zoe said. "I think the entire town believes you and Marius are about to get married."

"Santa's balls. I can't even buy a sandwich for the man who's helping to clear my name without the rumor mill cranking up? Marius is being nice."

"That blush says otherwise."

"Actually, he's being coerced by his aunt."

"Uh-huh."

"Yes, that's exactly it. He's going to go back to New York City after the holidays and forget all about me." I wrenched open the door to the café.

Marius was there next to the glass case, looking tastier than any of the cupcakes. He didn't seem at all like someone who would buy a voodoo doll of my deceased husband.

He couldn't be the killer, could he?

I did have terrible taste in men...

I smiled at him.

He didn't return it.

"We received the revised toxicology report back." He frowned. "With all the ingredients as requested. There's a complication."

CHAPTER 18
Marius

"I don't understand."

I ushered Emmie and Zoe into the kitchen storeroom for privacy and pulled out the paperwork I'd printed. "This"—I pointed—"is the report from a few days ago. From the cupcake Brooks allegedly was eating."

"The cyanide cupcake," Emmie confirmed.

"This one," I said, "was from one of the other cupcakes in the box. I asked the lab to test for ingredients."

"Egg, sugar, flour, butter." Emmie frowned.

"But," I added, "they also retested for toxins. And there was no cyanide in those cupcakes."

"So?" Zoe shrugged. "That just means the murderer didn't poison all the cupcakes."

"But they did," I countered. "Tetrahydrozoline. Found in medicated eyedrops. You can buy those over the counter."

"And I haven't bought any, so we just have to find out who did," Emmie argued.

"It's also in prescription eyedrops," I told her. "Everyone in the senior center uses medicated eyedrops. Therefore, a case could be made that you did kill him. Which is a problem."

"Emmie didn't." Zoe was furious. "And I can't believe you brought him a sandwich when he thinks you're a murderer, Emmie."

"I'm her lawyer. I have to—"

I winced as screams echoed from the main dining room of the café.

"Boss, help!" One of the blond Svensson girls threw the door open. "Someone's choking!"

"Call 911," I ordered as we raced into the Christmas-bedazzled dining area.

"Help her!" Cora yelled as Beatrice, hands around her throat, was turning purple. "I think she's choking. Help! Call the fire department!"

"Abbott, what the fuck are you doing?" Zoe demanded.

Abbott ignored her, taking photos of the chaos as Beatrice collapsed onto the floor.

Sirens blared outside as the fire department rolled up.

"I'm a doctor," one man announced, rushing to Beatrice, leaving a table where a stunned Rosie sat.

He felt her throat then pulled out an EpiPen and stabbed Beatrice in the leg. The swelling in her face immediately started to go down.

Beatrice gasped and gurgled.

"She needs to go to the hospital immediately," the doctor said to the EMTs who rushed into the café.

"Does she have any allergies?" I asked Cora.

"I don't know. I... We're not friends, really. We came in here to meet away from Oakley," she said tearily. "We figured she wouldn't come here."

"What did she eat?" I demanded.

"I don't... Uh... A sausage roll and a cupcake."

"The cupcake murderer strikes again!" Abbott said gleefully as Cora clung to Emmie.

"Get out," I snarled at him.

Abbott scurried away but not before snapping more photos of Beatrice. "I bet I can get one of the big TV stations to run my story." He was giddy. "Big Christmas bonus incoming."

"A woman almost died," I snapped.

"It's journalism," he said then started trying to interview onlookers, who were all too happy to give their crazy small-town opinions.

"It was an allergic reaction," Emmie was hysterically telling people who were anxiously looking at their food. "Everything is perfectly safe. See?"

I grabbed her wrist before she could take a bite out of the sausage roll that Beatrice had been eating.

"We need to have it tested," I said in a low voice as the police officers trooped up to jeers from the fire department that they were late as usual. "I'll handle the cops," I promised her.

"Are they going to arrest me?" she sobbed.

I hugged her tight and kissed her tear-stained cheek as her heart raced against mine and she took those horrible gasping breaths.

"I promise," I swore to her, "I won't let anyone hurt you. I'll handle this." I kissed her forehead and reluctantly released her.

"At least," I heard Zoe say as she led her sobbing friend away, "we know Beatrice isn't the murderer. No one's going to poison themselves, right?"

CHAPTER 19

Emmie

"I'm ruined," I groaned from the couch in the too-warm great room of the senior center.

Gran was plying me with alcohol and the box of cupcakes in fun flavors I was testing out. They all tasted like cardboard.

"Cora tells me you're being hysterical," Gran admonished as Cora came over with herbal tea for me. "There's a line out of your café. Everyone wants to see where Beatrice was almost murdered."

"Allergies!" I wailed. "She had allergies. The doctor used an EpiPen. No one was almost murdered today."

Gran shoved the bottle of Winter Wonderland tequila, which tasted about as vile as it sounds, under my nose.

"Drink up." She glugged the liquor into my mouth. "It still could have been a murder, you know."

"I thought you were on my side," I groaned as my grandmother tried to sponge frosting off my face.

"Emmie, are you all right?"

Marius's face appeared in my blurry vision.

"I'm ruined. Abbott just published a story about the cupcake murderer striking again." I waved my phone at him. "Also, he needs an editor. There are spelling mistakes. Ow!" I'd dropped the phone on my head.

Marius took it. "I just got back from the police station. It turns out Beatrice is deathly allergic to shellfish."

"So she accidentally ate shellfish at someone else's shop and had an allergic reaction at mine?"

Marius shook his head. "Someone in town—because of course this is a thing—has a pig that he uses to sniff out clams."

"Andy." I nodded. "He supplies Zoe's restaurant."

"There was shellfish in the sausage rolls... according to the pig, anyway."

I sat up. "But I don't use shellfish. And gross! Who puts shellfish in a sausage roll?"

"Don't worry about the mystery. You need to rest," Cora said, plumping up the pillows. "My grandmother says you woke up super early and were up all night."

"Good news sure travels fast here."

"You're going to have a nervous breakdown if you're not careful," Cora warned.

Marius sat down across from me.

I settled back on the couch cushions as the crowd drifted off to see what food Cora had brought.

I wiped at my eyes and took another swig of the tequila. "Sorry I fell apart. I'm not a good crime-fighting partner, am I?" I laughed weakly.

"Cora's right," the lawyer said seriously. "You've had a rough week." His large hand came up to trail through my tangled hair.

I was suddenly self-conscious about my disheveled state. I picked up another cupcake and took a bite. There was an explosion of orange and spice.

"This one is definitely going into the advent calendar for next week," I said, my tongue flicking out to follow the motion. "Look at that!" I showed him the cupcake. "It's, like, the perfect bite. I did good on this frosting." I was babbling, and he tracked the motion, like a cat with a mouse, as I sucked the frosting off my fingers.

Marius watched me, assessing, two fingers on his chin.

"Pro tip: Italian meringue buttercream is best if things are heating up. Swiss meringue buttercream, though—that stuff will wilt like no one's business."

Hazel eyes dark, they followed the motion of my tongue as I poked it at the frosting, testing the firmness.

"If you don't stop," Marius said in that deep voice, "I'm going to say something thoroughly unprofessional to you."

Panicking, I stuffed the rest of the cupcake into my mouth and chewed furiously. Though I'd been married, my sex life had started out lackluster and quickly swan dived off the cliff of mediocrity. Brooks had been my one and only, and eighteen-year-old me had thought the captain of the football team drunkenly fumbling me in the back of his pickup truck was the height of romance.

I picked up the tequila bottle to wash down the cupcake.

Marius grabbed it before I could open the cap. "I don't want to taste that tequila when I kiss you," he warned.

I licked my lips, tasting the sweet frosting.

What would he taste like?

"I thought you didn't want to get disbarred for sleeping with a client."

"I think we have enough evidence to prove that you didn't do it. You weren't at the scene of the crime when Beatrice was poisoned. Not to mention that the pig didn't find any other shellfish in your kitchen. I can make a solid case if I get dragged into the bar association for it."

"You lawyers. Always looking for loopholes big enough to stick your dick in."

His lips parted. A flash of teeth.

"That was the tequila talking," I croaked.

Marius leaned in, his breath hot as he lightly nuzzled my neck.

"I wasn't actually," he whispered as my chest clenched, "going to suggest putting my cock in any holes, loop or otherwise. I just wanted to do this." He pressed a kiss to my neck. "And this." Another to my chin. "And this." His lips feathered over my cheekbone and on the swell of my breasts.

"You fucking lawyers," I whispered against his mouth, dragging him up by his hair. "You're all so full of shit."

He grabbed my chin roughly, crushing his mouth to mine.

I clawed at the back of the wool suit jacket, wishing I could just tear the clothes off of him.

I should have left Brooks a long time ago if this was how it was to be with a real man.

His large hand slid down to my neck, forcing my head back so his tongue could plunder my mouth.

When he finally pulled back, I was panting against his broad chest.

Marius gazed down at me, eyes dark. Then he dipped his chin to give me another long, slow kiss.

Was this it? My ovaries were fired up and ready to go, and I had condoms in my purse because Gran was ever the optimist and regularly told me, "Fuck those marriage vows. You deserve cock in your life!"

After the pump and dumps by a drunk Brooks in the dark, I hadn't understood what she'd meant until now. And I wasn't going to be able to wait until Christmas to open my present.

"Do you want to go somewhere not filled with nosy old people so you can see if my pussy tastes as sweet as frosting?"

Startled, he widened his hazel eyes. I nipped his bottom lip as he strangled a surprised curse.

"I told you," I whispered, grabbing his jaw, kissed him, then pushed him back onto the sofa. "I want to thank you properly for saving me."

CHAPTER 20
Marius

Emmie was self-satisfied, cheeks flushed, when she met me outside the senior center. I was hyperaware of every little move she made as she sat in the seat next to me.

"Mm-hmm." She made that little moaning sound that led straight to my cock. "Heated seats." She wiggled.

My pants got tight.

"I almost," she said, trailing her fingers up the hand on the stick shift, "want to suggest you pull over here and show me how good you are at filling a loophole with that cock."

"You really sold everyone a bill of goods." I ground my teeth, trying to keep my eyes on the road and not on whatever she was doing with her hands in her blouse. "You're not a boring, sheltered cat lady."

"We cat ladies are freaks. Didn't you know that?" she purred as I pulled up the snowy gravel lane to the cabin.

I parked the car behind a copse of trees. Before I could turn off the engine, Emmie was straddling my lap. I pushed her back into her seat, kissing her, then moved down to take one hard nipple in my mouth.

"I'm not wearing any panties," she whispered, guiding my hand under her skirt and between her legs.

I couldn't wait for the cabin and didn't want to wait to find the key, unlock it, turn on the lights, warm it up—I needed her now.

You're not fucking her in this car.

The sheer force of willpower that had gotten me through a grueling three years of law school and the hundred-hour work weeks at Harrington-Thurlow law firm was the only thing keeping me from fucking her in the car and probably spraining something.

Emmie strained against me. "Fuck me," she begged. "Use me."

"Fuck." I slid my fingers against her soaking-wet pussy, sinking my teeth into her breast as I thought about my cock sliding into her *like that*. She was so slick and smooth.

"I cleaned up just for you."

"As soon as we get inside, I'm eating your ass out." I rubbed my fingers hard against her clit.

"So good," she slurred, gabbing my wrist and riding my hand, her whole body electric from my touch. She arched back against the seat as I slid a finger then another, into her pussy, feeling her clench on me as I finger fucked her and swallowed her moans with a kiss.

"I thought I was going to have to coax you into taking off your panties, but you're a greedy little slut, aren't you?" I growled as she gasped against me.

Her pussy lips were so swollen, her cunt so wet, her clit so hard that I practically came right there, thinking about that pussy clenching around my cock.

Her breath pitched higher. Panting and moaning. Her tits bounced on her chest as I added another finger plunging in her pussy, wanting to kiss her but also wanting to watch her come undone on my hand. I stroked her until she was coming, gushing all over the leather seat.

She guided my hand to her mouth, not breaking eye contact with me as she licked herself off my fingers. "Let me see it. I bet you're nice and hard."

"I told you," I growled, dragging her up by the hair before she could mouth me through the suit pants. "I'm not fucking you here."

I half dragged her out of the car, her blouse still undone under her coat as I kissed her, stumbling us through the snow to the cabin I'd rented for the express purpose of fucking that tight cunt until she screamed.

"You know." Emmie nipped my chin. "There is this one shifter book," she said, half draping on me, her hands pawing at my belt, "where the male panther chases his mate—this human girl he picked up from Waffle House—and then fucks her in panther form right there in the forest. It was magical."

"I'm sorry, what the fuck? You know, I used to volunteer at the ACLU, but I might need to rethink my position on government censorship. How is that even legal?"

She sank her teeth into the sleeve of my jacket. "And I want you to fuck me just like—"

"Shh!" I clapped a hand over her mouth as I saw movement through a window.

I pulled Emmie behind a massive tree. We watched silently as the front door opened.

"Oakley," Emmie hissed.

I nodded.

She was talking to someone, arms above her head, stretching and arching her back as she ran her hands through her hair.

"*You really know how to turn a woman into a slut,*" Oakley teased someone still in the cabin. Then she did some sort of salsa-dance-move thing on the porch, spinning in her high heels. "*Mama loves getting dick!*"

"It has to be Theo. I mean, who else could it be?" Emmie hissed.

But it wasn't the other lawyer who stepped out of the cabin.

It was Abbott.

"Oakley and Abbott? What the fuck is going on?"

CHAPTER 21
Emmie

I sat in the front seat, shocked, as Marius drove us down the forested country road.

"Abbott?" I asked. "But Oakley doesn't even know him. Like, Oakley was part of Brooks and Theo's little friends group. It was always Oakley and Beatrice and Theo over for parties, and I was the fifth wheel. Now we know they had some sort of weird circle-jerk swinger-sex thing going on. But Abbott?" I turned to Marius. "Weren't you friends with him in high school?"

Marius made a noncommittal noise. "We had some classes together."

"This doesn't make any sense." I stared out the window, willing the snowy forest to give me some sort of sign.

"Maybe..." Marius worked his jaw.

"What?"

"Never mind. The baby can't be Abbott's, can it?"

"No way," I said firmly. "I know Oakley. Theo is one thing, but Abbott... I mean, he's weird and a little nerdy— not that there's anything wrong with that. Nerds rule the world," I added when Marius stiffened. "But like, he is not Oakley's type at all. Unless..." I tapped my chin. "Is Abbott rich, do you know?"

"No. Whenever I was at his house, his mom didn't have much. Aunt Frances would always send me over with food. Abbott couldn't really spring for birthday presents or anything like that—not that we were invited to parties. He doesn't have money."

"So you guys were friends?" I asked.

There was that noncommittal noise again. "All I'm saying is he doesn't have money. Or a lot of sense."

"She's using him, then." I slapped the armrest.

Marius scowled.

"Hey! Barbie can be a doctor or an astronaut or a manipulative sociopath! Women can be whatever they set their mind to! We just need to figure out what Oakley wants from Abbott. Do you think you can talk to him? Please?" I begged, sliding my hand over his lap.

He white knuckled the steering wheel then made a hard right onto a snowy drive.

"How about," I said against his mouth, gripping his jaw as the car slowed, "if you interrogate Abbott, I'll let you act out your favorite porno with me?"

His eyelashes fluttered against my nose.

The car screeched to a halt.

"I think," he growled, grabbing my chin to kiss me roughly, "that you want me to act out your favorite unhinged romance porn scene with me."

He wrenched the door open, grabbing me before I could face-plant in the snow, then he easily flipped me over his shoulder. His gloved fingers were insistent under my skirt.

"Wait," I said to the back of his soft wool overcoat. "Where are we going?"

He just stroked me harder, the leather gloves rough in my pussy. Panting, I scrabbled at his back.

I heart a digital beep, then the snowy ground changed to stained wood. I was unceremoniously dumped over the back of an oversize leather couch.

"I got us another cabin." His fingers were still between my legs. "Take your clothes off. I want to see your tits," he ordered, still stroking me,

I kept missing buttons on my blouse as, hands trembling and trying to will my knees not to give out, I stripped off my top and my bra and kicked off my shoes.

He fisted a hand in my hair and bent me over the back of the couch, kicking my legs apart.

My skirt was bunched up around my waist as he continued to stroke me, working my clit.

"You know..." The deep voice had an edge to it. "This is actually the first time I've fucked a small-town girl."

Then I was coming on his fingers. Stars spun in my eyes as a man's jacket and shirt appeared on the couch by my head. My skirt came down and disappeared to the floor.

"Not much for a girl to do in a small town other than spread her legs for whatever shithead football player walks by, is there?" he continued.

God, this is going to be good.

"You sound like you need to work some resentment out," I goaded, wanting to feel well and truly fucked by his cock.

"Did the captain of the football team do this?" He trailed his tongue along the glistening slit of my pussy.

"Fuck," I moaned, my back arching. "What are you doing?"

"Seeing if you taste as sweet as one of your murder cupcakes." He chuckled, then his tongue was back in my pussy.

My fingers grabbed at anything I could reach as his tongue curled around my clit. I gripped his starched white dress shirt as his tongue dipped into my opening then higher, making me scream and jerk.

Marius grabbed my hips, his fingers bruising me as he spread me, his tongue everywhere. "You like having your ass eaten out, don't you?"

I could only moan as he lifted my hips up higher to really work me with his tongue, claiming every piece of me with his mouth until I was shuddering and coming all over his face.

I lay half draped over the back of the couch, barely registering the movement as a condom packet ripped.

I felt his cock, thick and heavy, against my thighs and moaned when he rubbed it in my pussy juices.

"You're going to be so fucking tight when I take you, Emmie." Then he spread me, that thick cock pushing against my opening, way bigger than anything I'd ever put in there.

"I don't think I can take it," I mewled as he ground his cock against my pussy.

"Too big?" the deep voice taunted.

"Yeah, I think—" Then I screamed a curse as he thrust into me, jerking my hips back against him as he plowed deep inside me.

A low moan escaped me as my pussy rippled around the thick length.

He didn't pull out, just leaned forward, that impossibly huge length shifting inside of me, almost making me come. He reached for my tits, one hand on each, and tugged the nipples, rolling them in his hands. "Can I make you come like this?"

"I, um…" I panted as my hips rocked back against him. One of his hands slid down my curves to my pussy, seeking my clit in the swollen slit.

"Don't make me come yet," I whimpered and pleaded as he stroked me, fingers hard on my clit, as hard as his cock in me. Then I was coming around him, moaning as he sank his teeth into my shoulder, trying to keep himself from coming in me.

"Fuck, Emmie." He pulled out, sending aftershocks of pleasure through me, then slammed into me.

My legs and hips thumped against the back of the couch as he took me over and over, his cock plunging deep inside me, hitting the secret spot until I was coming again, moaning his name.

He kept up the furious pace while I begged him for his cum, spreading my legs for him, taking every inch of that huge length until my hips ached.

Gripping my thighs, he angled me so he could fuck me deep and hard, my cries echoing around the paneled room until the pace got more sporadic.

"Come, Emmie. Fuck you—just fucking come."

He slammed into me again, then I was thrust into the storm of pleasure while he came inside me, milking every drop of cum into my aching pussy.

"Shit."

I was draped like a rag doll over the back of the couch as he slowly slid out of me.

He cupped my ass and gave me an affectionate slap, making me squeak.

"I'd give anything," he murmured, "to see my cum dripping out of that tight little pussy."

I could hear the high of the orgasm in the deep voice.

Well, then...

His footsteps faded while I tried to restart my brain.

That was sex? Damn. And they said it wasn't anything like the romance books.

I pulled myself up off the couch in time to admire Marius coming in with that Greek-god body, the muscles tight from sex, rippling under sweaty skin.

He handed me a warm washcloth and kissed me, hands cupping my face, as I toweled off.

"I don't know how any woman lets you go," I murmured against his mouth, running my fingers through his messed-up hair. "You fuck like an animal."

That earned me a slap on the ass and a nip of his teeth. "You read too much."

I dragged my nails down the washboard abs.

"I don't how any man would let you go." He kissed me noisily. "Kinky little slut like you. And no one else knows about it until I've got you with your tits out and your pussy hot and ready for my cock." His fingers slid between my legs briefly, affectionately. "You'd let me fuck you dirty, wouldn't you?" he murmured. "You're a little cum slut under all those sweaters."

His phone rang in his discarded pants. He squeezed my ass and answered it.

I slowly pulled on my clothes, the high of sex wearing off. I wished he would wrap me in a blanket and cuddle with me.

He's not your boyfriend—you just hooked up with him. He's leaving town soon. Better not to get attached.

Maybe I was just feeling the holiday blues.

The last time I'd been intimate with Brooks, it had been in a cabin just like this. Even though I'd said I was ovulating and wanted to try for a baby, he had insisted that he wanted to do an overnight trip with his friends. "Theo already booked the cabin!" he yelled at me.

I cooked a nice dinner that everyone complained about. The four of them all drank, and Brooks and Theo watched Oakley and Beatrice drunkenly dance in front of the fireplace while I refreshed everyone's drinks. I'd stood there as Brooks danced off-rhythm with Oakley.

I knew in my bones he and Beatrice had been sleeping together.

What if he'd been doing both of them at the same time? *Gross.*

That night, after cleaning up dinner and scrubbing the kitchen, I'd begged him to at least have sex so I didn't miss my window. Brooks had complained that he was too drunk and tired.

I bet he'd already had sex with them.

Oakley had been doing the same happy dance she'd done at the cabin earlier today and had been just as over-the-top affectionate with Brooks as she'd been with Abbott. I had wondered at the time if she was trying to steal my husband. Now I knew she'd already been sleeping with him behind my back, no condom whatsoever.

"Wait," I said slowly, my brain starting to draw parallels.

"What's wrong?" Marius's hand was warm on my back. "Sorry about that. Grayson called to complain I hadn't sent an email out yet."

146 · ALINA JACOBS

"Sorry, I know you have a real job," I said in a rush.

"This…" Marius kissed me. "Is more important, and what do you say I fuck that tight little pussy for another hour or so?" He nipped my lip.

I pushed him away.

He looked a little hurt.

I kissed him quickly.

"I'll walk you around on a leash and let you fuck me later, but first," I said, "I think I solved a big piece of the mystery." I clapped my hands. "She's not pregnant!"

"What? Who?" he demanded.

"Oakley. She was drunk earlier. You see?" I said. "She's been faking it. She has a fake belly. She's been faking pregnancy symptoms. That search on her laptop she did was probably looking for recipes she could make that would convince everyone she was nauseous and had morning sickness."

Marius was giving me a wary look.

I poked his broad chest. "You don't believe me. You think I'm crazy."

"It just seems really like a trashy soap opera plot or something. No one fakes a pregnancy. That's insane."

"Yes, but money and love make people crazy. I'm going to prove it."

I tapped my fingers on the armrest as we drove back to the first cabin.

Out in the snow on the stoop, I waited impatiently for Marius to look up the code to the door on the app.

It still worked.

"Come on, universe, I need evidence," I muttered.

Marius stood in the middle of the room while I ran around.

"Ah-ha! An empty bottle of wine in the trash can and two glasses in the sink, one with cherry-red lipstick. Oakley is lying! She's not pregnant."

CHAPTER 22
Marius

"I know," I said to Grayson as I walked to Girl Meets Fig to meet up with Zoe and Emmie after hurrying to finish the work I'd been neglecting. "I owe you those markups. But it's fucking insane here." I lowered my voice. The town had ears, and they loved to gossip. "There is a list of murder suspects as long as my arm, and everyone seems to be sleeping with everyone, and get this—one lady is faking a pregnancy."

On the other end of the line, there was a pause then a sigh. "I just think—Lexi, dammit."

Grayson's girlfriend came on the phone.

"What the frickety freak, Marius. That is crazy! I'm making popcorn right now. We want updates. All the updates."

"I want him to finish reviewing that contract—"

Lexi cut Grayson off. "Someone is *faking a pregnancy* with a fake belly and everything. Grayson, dude, you have got to live a little. This is gold! Small-town drama is the best drama. Maybe we'll get interviewed for the Netflix true crime special! Carry on, Marius!" Lexi chirped at me. "And give Moosey a kissy from me!"

The cat on my shoulder meowed at Lexi's voice.

Shaking my head, I stepped into Girl Meets Fig.

It was too early for the dinner rush, and Zoe and Emmie were sitting at one of the many free tables, heads together. The restaurant's decor was so different from when I used to work there back in high school. Less swamp witch meets HGTV and more upscale casual.

I was grateful for the change.

Though being with Emmie had taken the edge off of being in a small town, all the bad memories were bubbling up despite my best efforts.

Emmie looked up at me, eyes bright. Her lip caught in her teeth, like she was wondering if I was going to try to keep her a secret. As if I wasn't going to kiss her in front of everyone.

She melted into me as I tipped her head back to kiss her, maybe harder than I meant to, but I would happily say "Fuck it" to this murder investigation and spend the rest of December with her.

"Hi," Emmie whispered when I released her, my hand lingering on the back of her head. "Did you talk to Abbott?"

"Don't you have anything better to focus on than this mystery?"

She blushed as I stared at her. "What did you have in mind?"

"No!" Zoe slammed her glass on the table, making Moose hiss. "We're about to toss this Christmas wreath of cheaters into the fire," Zoe declared. "You guys can go hook up in the woods like teenagers after you clear your name, Emmie."

Emmie rubbed her hands together. "Oakley has a baby shower coming up. I think that's the perfect time to pull back the curtain and reveal that the wizard is a lunatic who lies about being pregnant."

"Didn't she just have a baby shower?" Zoe scowled.

"That was the family shower and the subsequent-close-friends shower. Apparently, this is the shower for third-tier people in her life."

"So we confront her then and put it all over the Facebook group?"

Emmie nodded. "We have to do it in a public place, or she'll just deny it."

"It's safer to wait for the baby to never appear. She won't expose her lie then. If," I warned, "she is actually faking it. She could just be drinking while pregnant."

"She's lying," Emmie said firmly.

"It's just an insane thing to lie about. I mean, she'd get caught eventually. She has to know that."

"Maybe she was going to steal someone else's newborn," Emmie suggested. "Oh, Cora was visiting Beatrice in the hospital with her granny. Maybe she has some insider knowledge."

"Tell her to come over here, and I'll give her free drinks and snacks if she tells us everything she knows," Zoe urged.

Emmie texted then set her phone down.

"Cora and Beatrice must have been plotting to take down Oakley. I bet that's what was going on in your café," Zoe said. "Oakley knew Beatrice was about to go all *Game of Thrones* on her, and she sent lover-boy Abbott to do the deed."

"We need to call her out now. We can't wait for baby shower number three or the birth. Someone else could get killed." Emmie looked concerned.

"Oakley was cheating on Brooks with Theo and is cheating on Theo with Abbott." I rubbed my chin. "There's no way Oakley is attracted to Abbott," I said, trying not to think of that fall in high school. "He must have something on her. She's not sleeping with him because she wants to."

Emmie nodded. "Maybe Abbot was rooting around for any detail he can put in his next article and came across evidence that implicated Oakley."

"But you said she was doing her happy-drunk dance. That's not what you do if you're having blackmail sex with the creepy town reporter," Zoe argued.

The bell over the door chimed.

"Sorry," Cora said, rushing over. "He followed me here." I winced as a flashbulb went off.

"Do you have a comment, Emmie, about what you're doing to keep people from being killed in the Santa Claws Café?" Abbott asked loudly.

The reporter took one look at me and blanched.

Emmie kicked me under the table. I knew she wanted me to talk to him.

I put on my best lawyer face and slowly stood up, buttoning my suit jacket.

"I did actually want to talk about the case with you, Abbott, if you have a moment."

"Well, sure," he said, fumbling with his camera and his bag and loping after me to an out-of-the-way table.

I was trying to find a way to broach the questions Emmie wanted me to ask, since apparently, the only way I was going to get to have her again was if she felt like progress was being made on the mystery.

The dinner rush was gearing up. More diners were arriving. Zoe was going to want the table soon.

I glanced to the door. Maybe I could stall and not have to revisit the past. I did a double take.

"Shit monkeys." Abbott's mouth opened comically, almost triangular.

Zoe zeroed in on her two newest customers, grabbing two menus as Oakley and Theo walked arm in arm into the restaurant.

Oakley had one hand on her lower back and one on her enormous belly.

"I, um... I actually have to go." Abbott tried to slide out of his seat.

I grabbed his shoulder. "What kind of reporter runs from a big story?"

Zoe and Emmie where whispering. Cora was standing awkwardly near the bar.

I didn't need a voodoo doll to get back at Theo and Oakley. My revenge had been delivered fresh from Santa's workshop and wrapped with a big red bow.

"In fact..." I raised my voice, projecting, like I was in a courtroom with half-asleep jurors and a hungover judge. "I would say this is the biggest story in Harrogate right now. Get your pen ready, Abbott, because it's going to be a killer of a news article. It'll be featured in every major news publication from here to Seattle."

The diners, happy to be getting entertainment with their meal, turned their chairs around to watch whatever was unfolding.

I paused for dramatic effect.

Oakley was the only person in the dining room pretending I wasn't there.

"What was the plan, Oakley?"

There were gasps from the crowd.

"You've been sleeping with Theo."

There were cries of surprise.

"I won't call it having an affair, since cheating on a married man is really just a pattern of poor behavior."

"Hear! Hear!" An elderly woman having an early dinner raised her wineglass.

Emmie grabbed Cora's wrist, watching me in horrified fascination.

"I'm here as her lawyer and a friend," Theo blustered. "I would never betray my best friend like that."

"Really? Because you seemed awfully concerned when you were notified of the last-minute change of his will. Did Brooks know you and Oakley were plotting against him?" I asked.

"Lies! Slander!"

"What I don't understand," I said, speaking over him, "is what was the plan? You pretend to be pregnant, Oakley, and—"

"You're not pregnant?" Cora screeched at Oakley. "You lied to Brooks about his baby?"

"What kind of sociopath are you?" Zoe added.

"There is a baby," Oakley said hotly. "I have a baby right here." She gripped her massive belly.

"In order to keep the house, the car, and the jewelry, you had to have a baby," I said. "And it had to be Brooks's. Surprise! Guess he didn't love you after all."

"I'm surprised you weren't digging up his corpse in the moonlight!" Zoe hollered, "To try to scoop out whatever was left of his rotting sperm to steal my best friend's house."

"You had no right to my house. What's worse is you weren't even trying to do right by your unborn child—you were just stealing from me. You and Brooks!" Emmie raged. "You plotted and schemed behind my back. You fed him poison about me."

"I just made him wake up and see you for who you really are—a dumpy, boring, piss-poor excuse for a woman and a horrible wife!" Oakley screeched at Emmie. "I'd say you were a horrible mother, but I know you can't get pregnant. You're defective. That's why your husband left you. That's why he didn't want you. You can't do the one basic thing any woman should."

"Brooks didn't want you either!" Emmie raged, tears in her eyes. "He was sleeping with at least two other women, probably more! You weren't special to him. He didn't like you, Oakley. He didn't love you. He didn't want a future with you. He was just using you for sex. The fact that he needed other affair partners tells me that you weren't even any good at it."

Oakley jumped up. "Shut the fuck up! I'm not you. I don't get cheated on."

"Admit it! Admit you murdered Brooks. Admit you faked the pregnancy. Admit it!"

I grabbed Emmie around the waist before she could lunge at Oakley.

"You and your fake baby!"

"Someone call the police! A pregnant woman is about to be killed by the cupcake murderer!" Theo bellowed to the crowd.

This was out of control. I should have had more self-discipline and not taken a match to this stick of dynamite.

"You ruined my life." Emmie was sobbing in my arms as I tried to restrain her from going after Oakley.

Moose darted through the crowd and launched himself at Oakley's belly.

Theo yelled obscenities, swatting at the cat with his napkin as Moose sank his claws into Oakley's belly. Instead of screams of pain, Oakley cursed as the pregnancy belly started to slide down her hips.

"It's the devil!"

One man fainted.

Theo was red-faced.

"Proof!" Emmie raged. "This is proof that Oakley is a murderer. And you're in on it, too, Abbott."

"No, I—"

"We saw you. Marius and I *saw* you two sneaking off into a cabin to fuck. You have proof of the murder—I know you do. Give it to me, Abbott." Emmie threw me off. "What do you have on Oakley?"

Abbot raced to hide behind me as Emmie chased him around the dining room while Oakley, shirt torn, tried to disentangle Moose from the fake pregnancy belly.

"Okay, okay!" Abbott said, breathing hard.

"Wait—you have proof Oakley murdered Brooks?" I asked, unable to keep the shock out of my voice.

Abbott squirmed. "Well, no… but I do have proof of the fake pregnancy."

Moose was now dragging his kill proudly through the dining room, tail held high as several people told him what a good cat he was, yes, he was, and so handsome too.

"We don't need proof. I already know she's lying about the pregnancy," Emmie said, fixated on him. "We need proof of the murder."

"How about estate fraud?" Abbott winced.

"Don't you dare," Theo warned. "What he's about to say is lies, and furthermore, I didn't have anything to do with it."

"Yes, you did!" Oakley screeched. "It was your stupid plan!"

"They needed a baby," Abbott explained, "and so I said that my parents didn't want to take my druggie sister's preemie because they already had five of her kids, and Oakley could adopt the baby then rehome it once she had Brooks's money in hand."

"But the paternity test…"

Abbott's shoulders sagged. "The newspaper isn't doing all that well. Print media is dying. I had to get a part-time job at the local lab. Svensson PharmaTech hires night contractors because they have a backlog of tests from a company they just purchased. Including paternity testing. I could fake the test results."

"For a price, of course," I murmured.

"Yeah!" Abbott was excited. "I told you way back when that the girls liked us, didn't—"

Theo fortunately cut him off. "None of what happened was a crime. No money changed hands. My client doesn't have any comments."

"No comments?" Emmie screeched, still incensed. "Well, I have a comment. You'd better get yourself and all your used condoms out of my house by the end of today, Oakley, and I'm going to enjoy all of my money. You won't see a dime of it. I'm getting all the life insurance, and yeah, it's a one-point-two-million-dollar policy, and I'm cashing it out, baby. Looks like the only person who came out on top of the cheater tournament is me! Joke's on you!"

Oakley and Theo ignored her, heading for the door.

"You had to have sex with Brooks for six months, and you got nothing! Not a cent! I get everything. You lose!"

"Emmie." I rested a hand on her shoulder. "It's over."

She turned to me, something sharp and dangerous in her face. "No, it's not. She needs to pay, just like Brooks did."

CHAPTER 23

Emmie

"I guess we shouldn't have had all those celebratory drinks," Zoe said later as I was groaning on the couch and sipping coffee.

Marius wasn't answering when I drunk dialed him.

"I think you freaked him out," Zoe told me and tried to feed me nibbles of flatbread pizza.

I loved arugula and goat cheese as much as the next girl, but when you were drunk and whiplashed, going from the greatest sex of your life to your dead husband's affair baby being fake, you just needed cheap, greasy pepperoni pizza to soak up the booze.

"I'm a rich bitch," I mumbled, trying to drag myself off of the couch to search for my phone. "I's a millionaire, and I wants a pizza."

"They don't deliver out here, remember?" Zoe said. "Because the horny seniors kept trying to flirt with the poor delivery boy."

Mrs. Roberts floated in, wearing a gauzy caftan. The old decor from Girl Meets Fig littered the walls of the small apartment in the retirement community.

"How were we supposed to know he was underage? Every male looks the same when they're under thirty-five, with those baby cheeks."

She inspected her reflection in the antique mirror on the wall.

I tried Marius again.

Emmie: *I'm sorry I scared you.*
Emmie: *I'll suck your dick if you bring me a pepperoni pizza.*
Emmie: *Extra-large.*
Emmie: *That's how I want your dick too.*

"Garlic knots," I mumbled, adding the request to the text message chain.

"Maybe a salad," Mrs. Roberts said pointedly.

"Marius didn't text me back," I flopped down. "So no salad or garlic knots."

"Marius! Now, speaking of jailbait, he did grow up into someone handsome, didn't he? I remember when he was a pimple-faced busboy. I gave him this special cream for his skin. Remind me to give you some, Emmie. I see you breaking out at your hairline. Weren't you two friends with him back then?"

"He was a grade or two above us, I think," Zoe told her grandmother as she hoisted my torso back onto the couch.

"And transferred to that fancy Connecticut private school." Mrs. Roberts drew a fake mole on her cheek. "After what happened to him, I don't blame him for leaving."

"Wait. What?" I asked.

Mrs. Roberts applied more lipstick.

"Oh." She smacked her lips. "He had bullies. They played some mean trick on him and his little friend Alfred. Mousy little boy. I'll always remember—I had come in Girl Meets Fig late that night, and Marius was there. He was so angry; he was washing off in the mop sink. I asked him what was doing there so late at night. He just looked at me and said, 'I'm going to kill him one day.' Then walked out, and I never saw him again. Heard he went to that boarding school."

That sobered me up.

"Kill who?"

But Mrs. Roberts was already drifting out the door. "I'm off to a séance, girls. We're communing with the Lady Alice's ghost that lives in the community theater."

Séance...

"Lilith. She said Marius killed Brooks."

"Grandma, wait—we're coming too!" Zoe yelled.

"Hurry along, girls. The spirit realm waits for no mortal."

"Marius couldn't have killed Brooks," I said as Zoe and I tugged on boots and coats. "He's not a killer, right?"

"The cards said you would return."

The seniors were pregaming with holiday sangria in the foyer of the community theater.

Lilith drifted like a ghost past us, face obscured in the dim candlelight.

We followed her into the dark theater. The doors thudded behind us.

"Now they want to know the secrets of the doll," Lilith whispered in the dark.

"Voodoo isn't real," I said.

"Then dig up your husband's corpse and remind him."

"Marius didn't kill Brooks," I said without much conviction.

"The will of a man with a thirst for revenge is unstoppable," Lilith said in a whisper. "It can topple nations. Surely it can snuff out the light of someone as weak as your deceased husband."

"Marius isn't a killer," I repeated, but I wasn't sure if I believed it.

"Anyone is a killer when they're pushed far enough." Lilith went silent.

I was suffocating in her dark eyes.

Like a snake, her hand whipped out, and she grabbed my wrist and pressed something cold and hard into my hand.

I looked down to see a little black stone cat.

"A talisman against evil men."

He doesn't look like a killer, I thought when I returned, shaken, to the senior living center.

Lady Alice did appear at the séance. She asked that the pigeons that were roosting in the bell tower be removed and said she didn't like the new neighbors—at least, according to Lilith and her Ouija board.

Marius capped his pen when I sat down across from him.

Though I'd been on a roll, confronting the potential murderer, this was the only time I'd felt nervous or afraid. I was very aware that we were alone in the room.

A log popped in the fire.

I flinched.

Marius's eyes narrowed.

Moose sat like a statue on the end table next to him.

Marius leaned back in the wingback chair, looking like the villain of a Victorian gothic novel. "Ask your questions."

It was like he knew, like he'd been waiting for me.

I licked my lips, wishing we could just forget all of this and he could just kiss me until we were willing to chance an encounter on the couch.

"Zoe's grandmother said…"

His eyes were unblinking.

"She said you, uh, threatened to kill someone a long time ago. She believed you meant it. Just tell me—was it Brooks? Did you kill Brooks with the voodoo doll?"

Marius set the Scotch he was drinking on the table. "Are you accusing me of using the occult to murder a man, Ms. Dawson? Do I look like a warlock?" He spread his hands.

Yeah, actually, he did.

"Lilith might be a witch," I croaked.

"I didn't kill Brooks, but he deserved what happened to him. I'm not sorry he's gone," Marius spat.

"What happened?"

Marius didn't answer, just looked at the fire.

I held my breath.

"Brooks had it out for me the minute he met me in kindergarten. No matter what my father and mother suggested—turning the other cheek, trying to fight back, ignoring him, trying to befriend him—it didn't work. I was his target. It got worse the older we got. Brooks with his little lackey, Theo, did everything and anything to make my life miserable."

I wrapped my arms around myself.

"Abbott was their other target. We hung out together for survival. I thought Abbott was my friend." Marius blew out a breath. "That is until that night. Abbott was all excited, told me that he'd been invited to a party and I could come too. I told him it was a bad idea. He insisted it was fine. That this girl Beatrice said she liked him. He thought he had a shot. He said her friend Oakley thought I was hot and wanted to hang out. We got there, and there were tons of people. Oakley acted like we were her best friends, the only people she wanted to see when we arrived. She gave us drinks, wanted to show us around, said she and Beatrice wanted to hang out with us, that they were tired of shitty jocks."

My hands were cramped from clenching them.

"Beatrice was waiting under this big oak tree. I was two steps away from her when I felt the ground start to give. I pushed Abbott out of the way as the ground collapsed, and I was buried in garbage. I thought I was going to die. The weight of it, the smell, was suffocating, and they were just laughing and laughing."

He shook his head. "I was so stupid. It was a setup, and Abbott was in on it. He was whining to Oakley and Brooks that he didn't think they were going to prank him too. They called him a—well, never mind."

"That's horrific!" I cried. "Your own friend betrayed you?"

"One thing you learn," Marius said coldly, "from seeing people during some of the worst moments of their lives, is that everyone has the capacity to betray the person they supposedly love. I've heard stories about people taking a hit for a friend or lover, but I've never actually seen it in person. It's human nature. Abbott fucked me over and got fucked over in return. Like Brooks and his pack were ever going to be friends with him." He stared at the fire. "It was fucking humiliating. And it shouldn't even matter." His anger was so tightly wound and controlled, just waiting to be released.

"Theo's been publicly humiliated along with Oakley. Abbott is a failure. Brooks is dead, for God's sake. I made it. I'm better than them. And it doesn't even matter. I'll never get over it." He stood up, brushing me off. "So yeah, I have motive to kill Brooks. I wish I had, honestly. But I didn't."

"That sounds awful." My voice was small. "Do you want me to kiss it and make it better? Or maybe you want to go have a drink get something to eat?"

"No. I should never have spent this much time here. I'm behind on work. Good night, Ms. Dawson."

CHAPTER 24

Marius

"**D**id you solve that murder yet?" Grayson asked.

I was exhausted. I hadn't slept that night—couldn't sleep, just stared at the pdfs on my laptop, stewing about the past, unsatisfied with whatever karma the universe had decided to hand out.

Living well is its own reward.

But it didn't feel rewarding.

"I—no," I said, rubbing my eyes, and poured myself another cup of the bitter coffee still out after breakfast had ended. "I think I'm going to go back early to New York."

"Your aunt will kill you," Grayson said, a hint of a smile in his voice. "She's hoping to convince you to find a nice girl, stay in Harrogate. The prodigal son returns. Did you take Emmie out to dinner yet?"

"More than that," I said, staring blankly out over the empty tables of the dining room.

"So he has found a reason to stay in Harrogate after all. And they say no good deed goes unpunished. All that pro bono work finally paid off."

"Yeah."

"Marius, rescuer of stray cats and damsels in distress."

Emmie wasn't a damsel in distress. Oh, she played one all right, but in the restaurant,

she hadn't been just angry. Hers was a vengeful, righteous fury.

In the cold light of the morning, after a sleepless night, my brain must have worked overtime on it because it made perfect sense.

"I think I know," I said slowly.

"What?"

"The murderer. I missed all the signs."

"But it's always the person you least expect," Grayson said.

"No. It's always the person you *most* suspect. Emmie killed her husband. She had means, motive, and opportunity. She had access to the drugs from her grandmother to kill Brooks. She gets revenge on her cheating husband and millions of dollars. She's the obvious suspect."

"You said she was innocent." Grayson's voice had lost any sort of softness. He was in pure ruthless-billionaire mode.

"I changed my assessment."

"Then get rid of her. Cut all ties with her," he ordered. "I know you said you were falling for her, but don't. If Emmie is the killer, you cannot be associated with her. My company cannot be dragged into this mayhem. Come back to Manhattan. Now."

I leaned back in my chair stared at the rapidly cooling coffee.

I should go pack. Should just leave.

What if I was wrong?

What if I was right?

If it were an employee of Richmond Electric, I'd advise them to cut off someone they'd only known a week if there was even a chance they could be a murderer.

I should never have gotten involved with Emmie and definitely should never have slept with her.

A chair scraped again the wood floor.

Emmie sat down next to me, anxiously twisting her hands in her lap. "How are you doing? I'm going to the Santa Claws Café, but I can send some food over for you." She reached out a tentative hand to stroke my cheek.

I jerked away. "I'm going back to New York City."

"I thought you were staying all December." Her big brown eyes were wide with worry.

"The CEO has called me back. Nonnegotiable."

"Really? What if I send him some cupcakes?" Emmie fretted. "I mean, I guess if you have to work, you have to work. I can come visit you. The train runs every—"

"No." I cut her off. "You can't."

"I don't understand."

"We can't see each other anymore, Emmie."

"Why? Because you're my lawyer?"

I turned my head to stare at her. "No, because you killed your husband."

Her mouth dropped open. "I told you I'm innocent."

"Yes. However, I'm a lawyer. People lie to me all the time. You have no idea how often people lie straight to my face."

"I didn't kill him." Shock and disbelief showed in in Emmie's eyes.

"You are the only one profiting from his death. You could have easily poisoned those cupcakes and gifted them to Brooks," I said. "This murder investigation and the little damsel-in-distress routine were just to throw me off my game. Even what we did in the cabin."

There were two angry spots of color dark on her cheeks.

"You seriously believe I was just using sex to distract you?" she choked out. "Who do you think I am?"

"I think you're a woman who wants to get away with murder and collect a massive paycheck."

"I can't believe you. We have all these other suspects—"

"What other suspects?" I snapped. "Rosie? Who else could it even be? Maybe your grandmother did it, hm? Maybe she's the real murderer."

I heard the crack before I felt the sting of her hand as she slapped me. "You, Marius, are an asshole, and I should have known because all you lawyers are vindictive, selfish pieces of shit." She stood up, the chair toppling. Her nostrils flared she stared down at me. "And to think I was starting to fall in love with you."

Grayson had decided I should be in Manhattan by now, back at my desk, and he'd been calling me nonstop.

I sat, stone-faced, in front of the fire in the sweltering great room as the windows darkened and Moose pawed at my leg, wanting to go outside.

Something wouldn't let me leave.

Part of me didn't want to walk away from Emmie, even if she was likely a murderer and was going to drag me down with her. Because once I got on that train, it was over. No more Emmie.

You didn't even like her.

But I did. Even though I tried not to, I did like her.

And she was falling in love with me.

Just to torture myself, I let my mind wander to a happy picture of Christmas in the future, in our home, with our cats and children, decorating a Christmas tree.

Instead, I was going to be spending Christmas alone in a cold glass tower far, far away from Emmie's warmth.

It was all a lie.

"What the hell is wrong with you?"

"Ow!" I yelped as Aunt Frances smacked me on the head with a rolled-up newspaper.

"How did you ruin it with Emmie?" she demanded. "You're going to end up old and alone. Moose is going to go find himself a little cat girlfriend and have a bunch of kittens, and you're going to be the creepy man with too many cats."

"I can't be with a murderer, Aunt Frances."

"Murderer? Emmie?" She snorted. "So what? Who cares?"

"My CEO cares." I looked up at her, incredulous.

"You need to tell him to mind his own business. Brooks deserved it after what he did to you. Did you tell your CEO that?"

"He doesn't care."

The elderly woman glared down at me. "I may or may not have sabotaged my cheating husband's riding lawnmower. Who knows? But you still come to visit your old aunt. You can't cut off Emmie for a little thing like murder. She's rich now! And she's hot. There are lots of widows around here much worse off."

"Aunt Frances, what the fuck?"

She pinched my cheek. "Stop poking around the murder, and stop all this foolishness. You're not going to find a better woman than Emmie—not with that cat anyway."

"I don't know…"

She shook her head. "You overthink things. You're just like your father. I should never have sent you to law school. You need a drink. Turn your brain off for a bit." She hustled away.

For a second, I wondered if the seniors had been the ones to off Brooks after all. They did have access to Emmie's cupcakes.

"Surely not…" I didn't want to pull that thread. I couldn't send my own family to jail, right?

Was she trying to tell me something?

Aunt Frances came back with a bottle of whiskey and a platter of cupcakes from the overflowing side table full of ever-multiplying holiday treats.

"Have a cupcake; you need a pick-me-up," she said, setting a platter of wilting cupcakes on the table after shooing Moose off it, and poured me a whiskey.

The cat meowed. I gazed absently at Emmie's cupcakes, listening to Aunt Frances whistle as she walked away.

I wondered if she was the murderer and maybe was poisoning me.

"You need to sleep, man." I downed the whiskey. "Aunt Frances wants me to have babies, not die. You're going crazy."

I poured myself another shot of whiskey and watched as Emmie's cupcakes wilted by the fire.

Funny—I'd never actually eaten one.

I picked up the closest one, red frosting with little silver candy sprinkles, like something you'd take to a holiday party. The frosting dripped onto my hands as I peeled the wrapper.

I stared at my fingers coated in red...

At the fire...

At the dripping frosting...

I stood up abruptly and went to the holiday table.

Under the croquembouche was a familiar red-white-and-green-striped box.

Emmie's cupcakes.

I carried them to my chair, opened the box, and set them next to the fire. I sipped another glass of whiskey as I watched the flames.

The frosting stayed firm.

Barely wiping off my hand, I left smears of icing on my laptop as I opened up the crime-scene photos, flipping through and zooming in on the cupcakes.

They all had wilted frosting.

"Fuck—they weren't her cupcakes." I sat back.

Fuck. I'd ruined it.

Fuck. Now there was a murderer loose... and potentially after Emmie.

CHAPTER 25

Emmie

After we'd closed up the cupcake shop, I said goodbye to the Svensson girls. Then I gave in and cried. Chin trembling, I began measuring flour for the new cupcake recipe I was going to test.

This was the worst Christmas ever.

I uncorked my bottle of baking cognac.

"Why do I have such terrible taste in men?" I wailed to the cats, who were certain they hadn't been fed in weeks and were starving.

Marius was probably in Manhattan in a fancy bar with a thin, pretty woman in a pencil skirt and garters, who was making bedroom eyes at him over five-hundred-dollar Scotch.

She'd never bake. All her bras and panties would match. She'd be able to go toe to toe with Marius on all his legal knowledge and make legal sex puns in bed.

Bet she didn't just lie there over the back of a couch while he did all the work. She probably did those expensive stripper classes on Thursdays.

"Kris Kringle's balls," I swore as I realized I'd lost count of the flour. "I just wanted to bake some cupcakes." I started sobbing and sank to the floor.

I couldn't get Marius's expression out of my head and kept thinking of how he'd accused me of murdering Brooks. Like he was so sure that I was an awful person.

Screw him.

I'd blocked his number immediately after leaving the senior center.

I'd also told Zoe to ignore him if he called her then begged her incessantly all day, asking, "Did he call? Did he email? Did he text you?"

No, no, and no.

Marius had walked out of my life just as easily as he'd walked in, leaving me with a mess to clean up.

To be fair, the rational part of me, which I was about to drown in alcohol, said Marius had technically provided thousands of dollars' worth of free legal help, gotten me out of jail, given me not one but five orgasms, and opened my café back up.

But still…

Now is not the time for being rational. Now is the time for drunk baking.

I hauled myself upright and rummaged in a drawer for a large spoon to start remeasuring the flour.

The smartwatch, buried under kitchen gadgets, buzzed right as I was shutting the drawer.

Likes Butt Stuff: *Are you really dead???*

Likes Butt Stuff: *You said you'd help me pay for my kids' holiday trip to Rockefeller Center. You still gonna do it?*

I took out my phone and dialed the number. "Who the hell is this?" I shrieked when a woman answered. "How many women was Brooks sleeping with?" The rage had settled in. "I can't get one lousy man, and Brooks had a whole harem of partners that he just rotated through. What the fuck? The audacity of men."

The woman cussed me out then hung up.

"How many more were there?" I snarled, scrolling through the smartwatch, cursing the teeny-tiny screen. "Rosie, Oakley, Beatrice, Tits, Likes Butt Stuff—was Brooks cheating on me with half the town?"

A YouTube video tutorial helped me access the threads of deleted messages, which let me find Rosebud in Training, Thick Thighs, and Fat Pussy because Brooks was nothing if not revolting.

Maybe that was why Marius had been so upset that morning. He was furious about Brooks—what he'd done to him—and he was hurting.

"It doesn't matter; he walked away from me." I took another long swig of cognac, to the yowls of irate and hungry cats, then furiously dialed each of the numbers of the women Brooks was sleeping with.

"Hello?" Rosie aka Rosebud In Training said. I recognized her voice.

"I know you slept with my husband!" I shrieked at her. "Homewrecker! And I'm destroying that bracelet."

"Emmie? What the—"

I hung up then punched in the next number and the next and the next.

Tits informed me that yes, she'd known Brooks was married, and no, she didn't care. She hadn't even wanted to sleep with him, but he'd helped pay her rent, and by the way, I owed her seventy-five bucks.

"My Christmas charity doesn't extend that far."

When I punched in the last number, Fat Pussy's, I almost thought I'd drunkenly mistyped because the name that came up...

"That can't be right." I shook my head. The noisy cats were giving me a headache. I stared out into the dark empty café. "Oh my God—I need to get out of here."

Feeling woozy, I hauled myself up. It took me several tries to unblock Marius's number on my phone.

"Pick up. Pick up," I muttered as I grabbed my purse, not bothering to fix the strap as I thrust my arms into my jacket. I made sure the back door to the kitchen was locked then scuttled to the front door, phone glued to my ear. "Pick up."

Ring, ring!

I froze as a ringtone echoed in the empty dining room.

Out of the corridor that led to the bathrooms, Marius slowly walked toward me, hands up.

Cora was behind him, holding a shotgun.

"Put that fucking phone down, Emmie," she spat, "or your boyfriend's going to be the second person to die in this shop."

"Don't do it, Emmie." Marius's voice was unnaturally calm for someone with a gun to his head. Probably all that courtroom training. "You hate me, remember, Emmie?" he said, giving me a crooked smile. "I was mean to you this morning. Just save yourself; I'm not worth it."

"Shut up!" Cora screamed, cocking the shotgun. "Get on your knees, and throw away that goddamn phone!"

Marius knelt down slowly. I dropped the phone and kicked it away.

"That's right. You took something from me, and now I'm going to take it from you," Cora said. Her voice had this creepy, unhinged lilt.

"I—what? Brooks was *my* husband. You were sleeping with my husband," I argued while Marius mouthed at me to shut up.

"No, he wasn't. He was mine first. We were together in high school. Brooks said," Cora sobbed, "that I wasn't as hard a worker as you, that he didn't want some gold digger. But..." She gasped. "I know, *I know* he loved me. I gave him my virginity. He had to love me."

"Are you sure? Because I'm sure this pattern of cheating behavior didn't just pop up out of the ground when he was in his midtwenties," I argued. "Brooks was probably juggling you and five other women. You and I are both victims. Just put down the gun. I'm sure we can work it out. I'm sure you didn't mean to kill him."

"You're not a victim. You're a villain. The only reason he's dead is because of you," Cora spat.

"Emmie didn't kill him—you did," Marius said, earning a rap of the gun on his ear.

"I may have pushed him off the ledge, but Emmie put him there," Cora snarled. "He was going to marry me." Her voice caught. "He said the other women didn't mean anything, that he'd made a mistake. But he could never just make a clean break. I just wanted to make him sick. I didn't mean to kill him. I just wanted him to realize that Oakley and all those other women wouldn't stick by him through sickness and in health. He wasn't supposed to die."

"What about Beatrice?" I asked.

"She lied to my face. She was sleeping with my man. She was in love with him. She told me that he told her they were going to be together, that he didn't like Oakley."

"So you put shellfish in her food?"

"Of course not! I didn't even know she was allergic. Karma got her with the allergic reaction." She wiped her teary face on her shoulder. "Even the universe agrees she had to pay for what she did. Don't you see?"

"All I see is a man who is not worth all this mess and drama."

"There is no man on this earth greater than Brooks." Cora was reverent. "He's charming and handsome and the captain of the football team. And his cock…"

"I've seen bigger," I said.

"Him?" Cora screeched, her attention back on Marius. I winced.

"Maybe I'll shoot that off first."

"Whoa," I said, trying to stall her. "I think there's been a big misunderstanding. Just put the gun down and walk away. No one is going to know that you were the one who killed Brooks. We won't say anything, right, Marius? You can finally be free, Cora."

"They'll know it was my grandmother's cataract medicine." Cora sobbed. "I'm going to jail."

"But…" I said, my mind racing.

"Stop stalling!" Cora screamed.

"You're not a murderer, Cora," I said urgently.

"Yes, I am! I killed the love of my life. I'll never be able to forgive myself."

"He died from cyanide poisoning. Your grandmother doesn't have cyanide in her medicine cabinet."

"But the eye drops..."

"Brooks didn't eat those cupcakes," Marius said. "We had tox reports done."

"I didn't kill Brooksey!" Cora sounded hysterical. The gun trembled in her hand, too close to Marius's head for my comfort. "But who...?"

There was movement outside of the window.

Rosie was outside, phone to her ear.

"She's calling the police!" Cora shrieked. The gun flailed. "I'm doomed!"

The door opened.

"Rosie, get back!" Marius barked at her. "You'll get hurt. She has a gun."

Rosie's face lit up. "Oh, Marius, I knew we had a connection." She sighed then blinked at Cora. "Cora, get that gun off of him, and shoot Emmie."

"What?" I choked out.

Cora hesitantly lifted the gun.

"I knew it was you!" I screeched at Rosie as she stroked Marius's face and hair then leaned in to press her lips to his. I saw red. "Get the fuck off of my man. Why are all of you trying to steal my men?"

Marius jerked.

Cora twisted the gun back on him.

"She's not, Emmie," he choked out, "I'm yours." Marius blinked rapidly, neck craning as Cora leaned the gun on him. "I just want you to know I'm sorry, Emmie. I'm sorry I didn't believe you, and I'm sorry I was mean to you. You're the best thing to ever happen to me, and I wish I hadn't thrown away the chance of you falling in love with me."

"Shut up!" Cora raged. "You don't know what love is. None of you know what real love truly is."

Rosie rolled her eyes.

"You murdered Brooks," Cora sobbed to Rosie.

"Of course I did. He had it coming. Now, where's my bracelet?" Rosie barked at me.

"You want a memento of the love of your life?" I baited her.

Rosie just scoffed. "As if. I'm not like dumb little Cora. Brooks betrayed me. He got what he deserved. I designed that bracelet myself, and I want it back."

I didn't move.

"Never mind. I'll fish it off your corpse." She pulled a tiny bottle of clear liquid out of her purse. "And replace it with this. Made it myself. Cyanide extracted from hundreds of apricot pits. We'll tell the cops that you admitted that you murdered Brooks for the life insurance money, won't we, Cora?"

Cora whimpered.

"If you don't cooperate," Rosie said sweetly to Cora, "and if you try and rat me out, I'm just going to tell everyone that you were an accomplice."

Something furry brushed past me. Out of the dark, they appeared—dozens of silent cats, led by Moose.

"But Marius isn't going to lie," Cora whispered and licked her lips.

Rosie looked down at him and ran her thumb over his lower lip.

"There's always another man. Pity, Marius—you're so handsome. Shoot him in the back, Cora, so we can have a nice funeral."

Cora lowered the weapon to his back.

"Please," I cried, "don't!"

Rosie startled when a cat rubbed against her boot, purring.

"Good kitty," Rosie cooed. "Such good kitties."

Moose, like his owner hadn't just had a gun to his head, calmly leaped onto Marius's shoulders and daintily licked a paw.

"I should have gotten a dog," Marius muttered as Moose jumped onto his head, totally nonplussed that Marius was in danger. The other cats slowly came over to investigate why a grown man was kneeling on the floor, jumping onto his broad shoulders like he was a cat tree, sniffing his coat.

Rosie laughed. "Dumb animals. They're just waiting for Cora to kill you so they can eat your corpse. Don't worry. Your new mommy will let you live in her new cat café. Cora, do it."

Cora racked the shotgun.

As if that was the cue, thirty pairs of eyes fixed themselves on Cora, then the mass of animals sprang.

I screamed as they attacked Rosie and Cora with teeth and claws, hissing and scratching.

The shotgun went off, and plaster rained down over us. Rosie screamed, and Cora tried to run.

My ears rang.

Cats went flying.

Cora fired again, blowing a hole in the wall, then dropped the gun as a tabby cat bit her on the hand.

Rosie was incapacitated on the ground, curled up as the cats, led by Moose, attacked her.

"Jesus Christ," Marius swore, sliding across the tile floor to scoop me into his arms and haul me to the door. "You have too many goddamn cats, woman."

CHAPTER 26
Marius

"I can't." The firefighters straight up refused to go into the café. "I don't get paid enough."

One of the firefighters had grabbed the gun before running back out into the cold to describe the horror scene in a panicky voice.

"On Facebook, they're saying the cats took her eyes," one firefighter said as his partner started to unwind the hose off the big red fire truck.

"You all are here," I argued with them. "You have more information than people posting on Facebook, and who is even posting? And don't spray that in her shop."

"Then you go call the cats off."

Bracing myself, I opened up the door and fished around for the light.

Cora and Rosie were still writhing and screaming as the cats bit and scratched them.

"Moose," I called, clicking my tongue. "Here, kitty kitty. That's enough—you're scaring the firefighters."

The Bengal cat hissed, ignoring me.

"Costco is still open, and I'll buy you all giant cans of tuna…"

That got their attention.

One pretty blue-eyed white cat with blood stains on her fur pranced through the café, purring, and rubbed against Moose, who seemed all too happy to let her clean him up.

"Dammit, I think I'm getting another cat," I said as the firefighters, squinty eyed, gave the cats perched on tables and chairs a wide berth.

The cats watched with keen interest as the EMTs loaded Cora and Rosie, moaning and bleeding, onto stretchers.

"Kris Kringle's balls." Emmie leaned against me.

I wrapped my arms around her and kissed her face, her hands, her mouth, her nose. "I love you, Emmie."

"You just met me."

"Nothing like a near-death experience to let you know what matters most."

She smiled up at me, her eyes sparkling. "Okay, that's it," she gushed.

"What?" I said, concerned.

"I just fell in love with you."

I kissed her.

"I'm never letting you out of my sight. And I'm going to kill the next woman who touches you," Emmie promised.

I kissed her hair. "I'm sorry. I'm so sorry I hurt you. Please forgive me," I begged, still holding her as tight as I could to my chest.

"I'm not mad at you. You had a lot going on." Emmie looked around at the mess. "I guess I'm closed for the season. This is going to be a nightmare to clean up."

A bus roared down Main Street. Firefighters dove out of the way, and the bus almost hit the truck and screeched to a halt. A stream of seniors poured out.

"Damn, I missed it," Emmie's grandmother complained.

"There's a good boy. You made up with Emmie!" Aunt Frances beamed at me.

The seniors immediately bustled in to start cleaning up the café.

"Just leave it. It's late; we'll never get it open in time," Emmie said from where she was slumped in a chair.

"The hell?" Edna yelled. "This is going to be the hottest spot in Harrogate in about twelve hours. You're my retirement plan, Emmie. Get a move on."

My great-aunt handed me a broom. "Unfortunately, you're more of a paper pusher than a blue-collar man, but many hands…"

A young man in coveralls I recognized from the retirement community trudged up the sidewalk with a toolbox, walked in, and sighed. "Granny, am I getting paid for this?" he complained.

An older woman pinched his ear. "How many times have I bailed you out of jail for fighting? I paid for your drywall certification, and you live on my couch. Get to patching, boy."

"All-you-can-eat cupcakes," Emmie promised him.

He perked up. "A murder cupcake? Hell yeah! Those are going for, like, twenty bucks on Ebay!"

CHAPTER 27

Emmie

"Do you think that this is in poor taste?"

"My aunt made me this sweater," Marius argued.

His red sweater was decorated with snowflakes and an anthropomorphized cupcake that had a dagger sticking out of it.

"I'm not the only one dressed up," Marius said, pointing at groups of people wearing various murder- and cupcake-themed items of clothing and eating the mini cupcakes I'd baked along with savory treats from Girl Meets Fig. "This party is to help raise money for your cat café franchise. You have to play up to people's expectations."

"This whole committee is going to hell in a handbasket," Gertrude complained loudly, walking by me, trying to collect donations for the pets-to-prison-pipeline project—working title—that Cora had started at the county jail with Rosie, who was shopping her story around for a Netflix special.

"Look at all the tickets we sold," I reminded her. "This money's going to help a lot of needy cats this winter."

Gertrude harrumphed. "That's because you were using sex to sell tickets."

"Let's see the goods, hot stuff!" Several drunk senior citizens whooped to Marius.

"Convince me to buy another raffle ticket."

"Striptease!"

"My adoring public awaits." Marius leaned in to kiss me hungrily, promises of good things awaiting me under the tree that night.

"If that's how he kisses, I'm gonna buy the whole book of tickets," Ida declared.

The band, consisting of several of the local high school boys, played the last few chords of an enthusiastic rock and roll rendition of "Silent Night."

On stage, Marius pulled his sweater off, shaking his head. His hair, not combed down like it normally was, fell over his forehead. He tossed the sweater into the audience to screams for the seniors.

My heart fluttered.

"Thank you for coming and supporting a cause dear to my heart," Marius said into the microphone one of the teens handed him. "Each party ticket does come with a raffle entry, but buy more! You could win a date with me at the infamous murder cat café, for cupcakes and coffee."

"I'm going to have to change the name, aren't I?" I sighed.

"And maybe you'll even adopt a feline friend," Marius continued on stage. "I adopted my second cat from the Murder Cupcake Café."

"You literally sleep with him," Zoe reminded me before I could reach for my wallet. "You don't have disposable income to spend on extra raffle tickets for a date with your own boyfriend."

"Last chance to make sure you've got your raffle tickets, everyone. The drawing's going to be in fifteen minutes."

When Marius loped back to me, he held out his hand for his sweater.

"Uh-uh." I trailed my fingers up those washboard abs and rested my chin on his broad chest. "I like you just like this."

People dumped money into the Santa-hat bucket I carted around to collect last-minute raffle sales.

"It's too bad. I was hoping Oakley was going to be here. I wanted to see where she bought that baby bump," Ida was saying as I counted out her twenty raffle tickets. "She cleaned up real good at those baby showers."

The band started playing "All I Want For Christmas Is You" as Alice took the giant bin full of raffle tickets up to the stage.

She made a big, dramatic show of pulling out a ticket.

"Number eight two three four. Who has that ticket?"

A few yards away from me, a tall brown-haired man with green eyes raised his hand.

"We won, Marius!" Lexi screamed as Marius's boss held up the ticket.

"You're going on a date with your boss?" I snickered, nudging Marius.

Zoe waggled her eyebrows at him. "I'd pay to read that romance novel."

"Aww, you bought a ticket, Grayson?" I said when he walked toward us.

"Can we convince you to take a cat?" Zoe added.

Grayson smirked and slapped the ticket in my hand.

"Merry Christmas."

"But it's my café and my…" I gestured helplessly at my boyfriend.

"I need you to speed up the dating process," Grayson said matter-of-factly.

"We're going to have children soon," Lexi gushed.

"And I'd like for our kids to grow up together, Marius," Grayson added.

"So get busy, you two!" Lexi broke open one of the sprinkle-filled Elf-Fetti cupcakes over my head, showering me with sprinkles. "This is my favorite cupcake yet! You need to ship these advent calendar cupcakes nationwide!" the short redhead told me.

Marius leaned down to kiss me again. "What do you say? You want to go on a date?" He nuzzled my neck. "You know, I have never actually tasted one of your cupcakes."

"Seriously, Marius?" His great-aunt swatted at him with the bunched-up sweater. "I thought I taught you better than that. Be careful! If you don't do oral, she might just murder you!"

EPILOGUE
Marius

My daughter gave us a confused look as we finished singing "Happy Birthday to You."

"Eat some cake," Emmie coaxed.

Grayson's daughter toddled over and shoved her friend's face into the cake.

"That's not how we treat friends." Lexi scooped up the little girl.

I held my breath, waiting for Millie to cry, but she just clumsily licked frosting off her fingers.

"I have actual cupcakes for the adults to eat." Emmie whisked out a tray.

My parents, tanned from their cruise, took pictures of their granddaughter while my sister wanted to know when her baby could open presents.

"I'm officially in my cool-aunt season," Elizabeth declared.

Millie didn't seem that interested in the presents, content to chase her friend around with the washcloth.

"You still salty Marius didn't take over the practice?" my sister joked to my father.

"I am. To see my great-grandniece, I have to take a train all the way to New York City," Aunt Frances declared.

"No, you don't. We're not even there that often," I argued.

My dad snorted.

"What?" I asked, trying not to be testy.

"You weren't going to take over my practice. I like having someone in this family who makes money. Pays for your aunt Frances." He grinned at me and patted me on the back.

"Come. Make her open presents," my sister begged me.

Millie was over in the cat food bowl, trying to eat the kibble.

Moose licked her face. He loved my daughter, but Princess, the white cat, was very much Millie's cat.

The big Persian walked next to my daughter as she toddled around the yard, nudging her when she got off course.

My sister finally plopped down next to her niece and started to help her open the presents, with Grayson's daughter also ripping at the fancy wrapping paper.

The first present...

"Why did you give her that?" I asked Elizabeth.

"What? It's cute," she said, holding up the cupcake stuffie with a two little Xs for the eyes. Grayson's little girl grabbed at the stuffie with frosting fingers.

"We bought her books, dear. Don't worry," my mom said to me as my sister helped Millie unwrap what looked like a very noisy toy.

"Why don't you unwrap one of mom's presents?" I told my sister.

Elizabeth rolled her eyes and handed Millie a flat package.

She promptly started chewing on it. Then, coaxed by Elizabeth, she was finally able to unwrap it.

"A murder-cupcake book?" I sighed.

"I made it myself!" My mom was giddy.

"Ooh!" Emmie had said we should sell those in the store.

"Murder Cupcake does pay the bills," my dad joked.

It was a franchise now. Emmie did a brisk business during the holidays. The cupcake advent calendars were a popular item. Halloween was the second most profitable time.

"All she wants is the wrapping paper," Elizabeth complained. "I should have just saved my money and wrapped an empty shoebox."

"Scoot in for a photo," my mom coaxed.

Emmie wrapped her arms around my waist.

"I love you." I leaned in to kiss her.

"I love you so much more than I ever thought," she murmured.

I rested my head against hers for a moment. "One whole year."

"Let's do it again!"

"Let's have another baby?"

"No—all of it! The first meeting, the sex in the cabin..."

"The murder cupcakes?" I tipped her head up.

"I am working on a new recipe!"

ACKNOWLEDGEMENTS

A big thank you to Red Adept Editing for editing and proofreading.

And finally a big thank you to all the readers! I had a great time writing this hilarious book! Please try not to choke on your wine while reading!!!

About the Author

If you like steamy romantic comedy novels with a creative streak, then I'm your girl!

Architect by day, writer by night, I love matcha green tea, chocolate, and books! So many books...

Sign up for my mailing list to get special bonus content, free books, giveaways, and more!

http://alinajacobs.com/mailinglist.html

Made in the USA
Middletown, DE
10 December 2024

66555759R00117